A HEARTSONG BACK TO THE HIGHLANDS

RONAN'S STORY

A MACKAY CLAN LEGEND - A SCOTTISH FANTASY ROMANCE
BOOK 2

MAEVE GREYSON

This is a work of fiction. Names, characters, places, and incidents either are the product of the author's imagination or are used fictitiously, and any resemblance to actual persons living or dead, business establishments, events, or locales, is entirely coincidental.

A Heartsong Back to the Highlands

COPYRIGHT © 2024 by Maeve Greyson

All rights reserved. No part of this book may be used or reproduced in any manner whatsoever without written permission of the author or Author Maeve Greyson LLC except in the case of brief quotations embodied in critical articles or reviews.

NO AI TRAINING: Without in any way limiting the author's [and publisher's] exclusive rights under copyright, any use of this publication to "train" generative artificial intelligence (AI) technologies to generate text is expressly prohibited. The author reserves all rights to license uses of this work for generative AI training and development of machine learning language models.

Contact Information: maeve@maevegreyson.com

Author Maeve Greyson LLC

55 W. 14th Street

Suite 101

Helena, MT 59601

https://maevegreyson.com/

Published in the United States of America

To those who believe without seeing...

CHAPTER 1

"Ronan," Dagun roared. "Today? Be today the day we die?" Ronan laughed at his first mate's panic that the wind and driving rain carried to him from across the ship, then off into oblivion. Poor old beggar. Dagun had endured many a storm at sea, but this one appeared to be a bit too harsh for his liking.

The deck dipped, then lurched upward with the wild fury of the angry waves. The crew struggled to hold fast, but they tumbled and flailed from pillar to post, as if they were naught but a wee bairn's rag doll. Dagun tangled his arms in the rigging to keep from slamming into the ship's railing—or worse—be tossed over the side and swallowed by the churning sea.

"Clíodhna willna harm us," Ronan bellowed to them. "She's but bouncing us about for a wee bit of fun." More at home at sea than on land, he stood easy at the wheel, his stance wide and balanced as though the vessel was naught but a gently rocking cradle.

"Aye, then," Dagun sputtered and coughed after a wave hit him full in the face. "I be mighty glad about yer certainty of the sea goddess and her many moods—be they foul or be they fair." Another salty blast knocked him off his feet and left him dangling from the rigging.

Ronan flashed a smile at the deluge's sting and the lashing bite of the wind. His pulse quickened with each swell and heave of his beloved waters. A hearty laugh rumbled from deep in his belly and joined the song of the howling gale. His spirits soared as the black thunderclouds stirred like a boiling cauldron about to overflow. Fear of the storm would never plague him. Not here in his home. In the arms of his untamable ocean. His beloved Sea Goddess Clíodhna had won his loyalty and trust long ago when he was but a wee babe in his mother's arms. The goddess had appeared to him in the form of a selkie that day and taken many forms since, always striving to amuse him and show how much she cherished him. Clíodhna would let no harm come his way.

He never questioned the mystical ways of the goddesses or the powerful energies flowing through his world. Conceived in the dream plane, his mother a powerful twenty-first century witch, and his father a time traveling Scottish laird from the fourteenth century, magic filled his blood. The Goddess Brid herself had named him, for his destiny was to have dominion over the sea and every creature in it. A wee storm stirred up by Clíodhna was tonic to his very being.

"Douse canvas!" Dagun roared into the hurricane while squinting up at the creaking mast straining against the force of the gale. "She canna bear much more of this wind!" If they didn't get the sails dropped quickly, the mast would surely snap and drag them into the unforgiving depths.

Ronan shook his head as his terrified crew staggered across the deck. Their expressions revealed their unspoken prayers and fears that they would never see home again before they died.

"Clíodhna!" he shouted into the wind. "Leave off and move on to pester some other unsuspecting mortals. Ye have frightened my men long enough."

The storm died like a snuffed candle. Mountainous waves smoothed to subtle ripples. The sun broke through the thinning clouds scurrying across the horizon. A rich golden voice floated on the breeze and danced across the water.

"My beautiful Ronan," it said, "ye ken I was merely having a wee bit of fun."

"Aye, my goddess, and ye ken how I enjoy a hearty storm." He cast a smile up at the fluffy white clouds tumbling across the brightness of the clear blue sky. His long hair, black as the ink of a squid, quickly dried in the gentled wind as the Goddess Clíodhna breathed a warm balminess into the air. He winked, even though she had yet to take solid form. "Ye are wondrous, my goddess, but I fear the fury that charges my blood with exciting energy drains the marrow from my crew's bones."

A mighty wave crashed over the railing, its sparkling white crest transforming into the shapely figure of a striking woman. Her white hair swirled around her enticing curves and puddled around her feet. Her translucent skin gleamed in the sunlight, iridescent as a pearl pulled from the sea. She was clad in a delicate clinging garment colored with the hues of the waters, rich sapphires, emeralds, and aquamarines. The gown shimmered and changed with her every move. When Clíodhna took human form, she ensured that the form she took was breathtaking.

The goddess smiled as she touched his cheek with the tenderness of a lover's caress. "My precious Ronan. Ye ken I treasure ye and will always see ye safe. No one adores my beloved seas like ye do. 'Tis such a pity ye are but a wee mortal, fragile as a bit of driftwood. Ye would make such a fine god, a wondrous immortal, and consort."

He covered her hand with his and chose his words carefully. "Ye ken I honor ye, and the seas shall always sing to my heart and soul. But as ye say, my beloved goddess, I am but a mere mortal—and that canna change."

She narrowed her stormy blue eyes but kept her smile in place as she leaned forward and brushed a motherly kiss to his forehead. "Ye are a wise little mortal as well, choosing yer words with such care. Have ye spent time with Brid again or has yer wee brother, the fox, given ye lessons on slipping through snares?"

Ronan ducked his head, feeling guilty as a lad caught stealing sweets from the pantry. The mighty Brid had warned him to take care with whatever he said to Clíodhna, for she was known for twisting a man's words when granting their wishes. Often, she turned a mortal's most cherished dreams into unimaginable nightmares. Of course, conversations with the all-powerful Brid also took careful wording. But he was extra wary with his precious Clíodhna of the seas.

"As I said," he assured her, "I will honor ye to the grave."

Her laughter bubbled like the gurgle of water as it poured from an urn. She combed her fingers possessively through his tangled mane. "My dear sweet Ronan. What more could a goddess ask for? When I look into yer heart, I see a soul so devoted and pure that it takes my breath away. Ye shall always have my protection, my handsome mortal. Always."

He bowed his head in reverence. "I thank ye, my goddess, for calming the storm."

She returned to her realm in the next wave that swept across the bow.

The crew shook their heads, their relief apparent as they returned to their duties. With the temperamental goddess no longer in their midst, they hurried to repair the damage from the storm.

Ronan watched them from the wheel, well aware they had heard the rumors about him before signing to serve on his ship. His mystical powers and dominion over the sea were not a secret—at least not upon the waters where he felt most at home. A smile came to him as he remembered one of them confessing they had not truly believed until they'd witnessed his easy relationship with the sea goddess, and how she calmed any storm with just a word from him. They were a superstitious lot. That, he knew, but he hoped they all felt him to be the safest captain to sail under. After all, if the sea goddess kept him safe, the mighty Clíodhna would keep them safe as well.

He turned back into the wind and gave the wheel a gentle turn. Without the storm to distract him, the nagging twitch that had troubled his soul of late demanded his attention once more. He scrubbed his chest, wishing he could rub the annoying strangeness of the ache out of his being. Being the middle son of the MacKay laird, it could not be the curse that demanded he find the other half of his soul. But if not that malady, then what? He rolled his shoulders and flexed his back until it popped, but still, the sensation persisted. A subtle gnawing made his heart ache with longing. Something pulled at him, nagged him to find whatever it was, and claim it for his own.

He snorted and rolled his shoulders. Whatever the feckin' problem was, he fully intended to ignore it. He refused to look for trouble. After all, whenever trouble wished to find him, it always managed it easily enough on its own.

"Mama, I still canna see him." Aveline, youngest of the MacKay brood and the only daughter, landed a petulant kick on the oversized slab of limestone that protected the heavy oak floor from stray blasts of errant magic. She stared harder at the large, imageless mirror leaning back against a stone wall blackened by ages of soot from its powerful energy. The obsidian surface showed neither reflections of the room nor the visions of her brother she had tried to call forth. Why did the Mirrors of Time always obey Mama's commands but more often than not ignored her? Maybe if she invoked Mama's name? "Stupid thing. I am just as powerful as the mighty Rachel MacKay. Do as I command ye!"

"Aveline, stop behaving like a child. You're a young woman now, and throwing tantrums gets you nowhere. Now, concentrate as I taught you." Rachel MacKay, mother to the MacKay brood, looked up from the worktable, pausing with her quill above the large book laid open in front of her. Even though her ebony hair glimmered with silvery threads of gray, she was still a striking woman who drew admiring looks from every man she encountered—but only if her husband wasn't around. No man who valued his life dared to allow his glance to linger overly long on Laird MacKay's beautiful wife. Aveline wished she had her mother's coloring and beauty—instead, she was cursed with reddish blonde hair and freckles that made her look as though the Goddess Brid had sprinkled her with spices.

Her mother rose from her seat and brushed the wrinkles from the apron tied around her narrow waist. She eyed her work, then glared at Aveline. "I should have known better than to attempt an update to a complicated text while you worked on your lessons." Her glare became more pointed. "Or whatever it is you are doing. What are you doing?"

"I am looking for Ronan." Aveline refused to feel guilty about worrying about her brother. Her mother just didn't understand. Ronan needed to come home—and not just because she missed him. He needed to come home and stay. She wasn't sure why, but she felt it deep in her bones. "Have ye not always told me to listen to my instincts?"

"Yes, my girl. I have at that." Her mother placed the lid on the inkwell and moved the quill away from the table's edge. She shook a finger at the cat eyeing the long feather with interest. "No, Midnight. Do not do it."

The feline blinked its great golden eyes and flipped the end of its tail as if laughing at her.

She moved behind Aveline, tucked her daughter's reddish blonde curls behind her ears, then took hold of her shoulders and pointed her at the mirror. "Remember what Emrys and I told you. Hold Ronan in your mind and call out to him. Envision him and soon you should see where he is and what he's up to."

"I did that already. It's not working." Aveline scowled at the infuriating mirror that refused to cooperate. Her mother needed to take her seriously. "He has never been gone this long before," she said, "and there have been more storms this season. Bad storms. Something is wrong. I feel it. What if something happened to him? I hate it when he's out to sea. What if—"

"Aveline, stop! I will not tolerate such talk!" The thunderous energy in her mother's voice made the jars of herbs lining the shelves tremble until they came close to rattling off onto the floor. Whenever Mama's emotions were stirred, her powers amplified everything she did. "I would know if something ill had befallen him." She pressed her fist to her chest. "I feel each of you. Ronan is safe. But as soon as that inconsiderate rascal does return home, I'll have a piece of him for causing me all this worry. Mark my words!"

With a glance at the mirror farthest to the right, Mama intoned the command. "Ronan MacKay, show me your place. Show me your ship. Show me your face. Show your mother where you roam. Do not make me bring you home!"

Aveline held her breath to stifle a victorious giggle. Thank goodness, Mama had finally chosen to get involved. Most days, Aveline was the one always in trouble with Mama or Papa, or both, since she was the MacKay offspring most often found at the keep. Youngest of four and the only girl, she had the worst of it when it came to which MacKay child got away with breaking all the rules. Unlike her brothers, whose antics rarely drew anything more from her parents other than a roll of their eyes, a shake of their heads, or laughter, she never got away with anything.

As soon as the echo of her mother's commanding spell faded, her brother's handsome face appeared in the mirror. Aveline so wished she had her mother's powers. No one and nothing ever questioned Mama's word.

Ronan's black hair whipped in the wind even though he had attempted to braid it back out of his eyes. What looked to be a brisk breeze filled the sails behind him. His dark green eyes narrowed as he looked toward the horizon. His broad smile, made lop-sided by the one dimple in his tanned right cheek, gleamed bright and true.

The sight of him healthy and hale made Aveline smile and breathe easier. He looked so much like Papa. Viking blood ran strong in the MacKay men's veins. It was obvious by the sheer massive size of them. Papa stood well over six and a half feet tall, and his three sons were his equals. But where Papa was blonde, Ronan was dark like Mama.

"Where are you, son?" her mother asked as she arched a brow at Ronan's image.

"I will be home soon, Mother. I promise ye."

"You promised me that three moons ago, boy. Where are you?"

"Mother—'tis unimportant where we are."

"Do not make me bring you home. Where are you?"

"Now—Mother." Ronan's voice took on a pleading tone.

"Aveline misses you. She needs her brother here."

"What about Latharn and Faolan?"

"She sees them regularly and knows them to be safe. Unlike you. She hates it when you're gone this long. Do not make me bring you home." Thunder rumbled off in the distance, adding strength to her command.

"Yes, Mother. I shall set course for Scotland immediately."

"You are a good son."

"I love ye, Mother."

"And I love you, Ronan, and look forward to seeing you soon."

"As I look forward to seeing ye," he said, then his narrow-eyed gaze shifted to Aveline. "And the wee bratling who made me the target of yer ire."

"I love ye, Ronan," Aveline called to him, knowing full well that he would never stay angry with her very long.

"I love ye also, my wee bratling, and will see ye soon."

CHAPTER 2

Harley stacked the dinner trays onto the trolley and noticed that, once again, Mrs. Neeley hadn't eaten a thing. That poor little old woman was going to waste away to nothing if she didn't start taking in some food. "There has to be something we can do to get her to eat."

Nurse Rosa glanced up from the charts where she recorded everything the residents consumed, be it solids or liquids. "If you can think of a way to get that little sweetheart to eat, then you truly are the miracle worker everyone says you are."

Harley frowned down at Mrs. Neeley's untouched tray. The unappetizing smell of overboiled and unseasoned green beans, what might be carrots or yams, and a mound of brownness that did not resemble the chunks of beef listed on the menu sheet hit her full in the face when she lifted the clear plastic lid.

"Wow." She wrinkled her nose and braved another hesitant sniff. The food wasn't bad, but it wasn't good either. She barely dipped her little finger into the pale yellow pudding and touched it to the tip of her tongue. "Yuck." She hurried to replace the cover over the mediocre meal. "I would have to be starving to be thankful for that plate. How many diet restrictions is she under?"

Rosa flipped to Mrs. Neeley's chart and squinted through her reading glasses as she tapped the ink pen against the board. "No salt, sugar, fat, or dairy. No gluten—and very little red meat." She shook her head. "Bless her heart. With all these restrictions, she'd find cardboard tastier than the recommended meals we serve here."

"She's ninety-six years old. The woman should be able to eat whatever she wants to, for heaven's sake. Who wants to live forever?" Harley snorted a disgruntled huff as she pushed the trolley full of dirty dishes into the kitchen and began loading the industrial-sized dishwasher. If she lived to be ninety-six years old, she was going to eat whatever she wanted. Anyone trying to restrict her diet could just kick rocks.

"You better not let Dr. Langerson hear you talking like that." Rosa pushed her dietary chart cart into its cubby at the end of the counter and locked the wheels in place. "These old folks are a gold mine to that man. He intends to keep them alive and kicking as long as possible."

"I want to keep them alive and kicking too, but, my gosh, there is such a thing as quality of life. If I'm ever doomed to living on a case of pills, eating tasteless food, and rooming in a sterile, lonely environment—then hand me a gun and make sure it's loaded, so I can be on my way to a better place."

"Harley! What a thing to say." Rosa made her usual scolding sound, clucking her tongue like a ticking time bomb, as she trundled out of the kitchen to hand out the evening meds.

Harley flipped her long dark ponytail behind her shoulder as she clicked the door shut on the dishwasher and started it with a spin of the knob. She didn't care what Rosa thought about her belief in living and dying. While it was important to take care of yourself and be as healthy as you could be, it was foolish to make yourself miserable and drag out that state of being miserable for as long as possible.

She rinsed her hands, dried them off, and returned the kitchen towel to its bar on the counter. An urge to help poor Mrs. Neeley nagged at her like the gnawing of a headache that refused to be ignored. "I will find her something tasty if it's the last thing I do." She yanked open the refrigerator door and sorted through the contents in search of something delicious and tempting. "None of this would tempt me. Moving on." She closed the door and went to the freezer, pawing her way through the frosty goods. Surely, there was something tasty hiding in here. She flipped over a bag of peas and spotted a hidden treasure. "Jackpot. This will be perfect."

Rosa's granddaughter had been to visit and loved orange sherbet popsicles. One of them was still in the freezer. It wasn't sugar free, but that was okay because Mrs. Neeley was not diabetic. Not dairy or fat free either, but the dear old lady had never had issues with either of those things. Rosa said the doctor just automatically put everyone on those restrictions. The popsicle was totally illegal and perfect.

"Okay, let's put this in a bowl, and then we'll sneak it to her." She pulled a small plastic bowl from the cabinet and a spoon from the drawer. As she made her way to Mrs. Neeley's room, she softened the sherbet off the stick and into the bowl. A glance down the hall made her quicken her step. She wanted Mrs. Neeley to have enough time to enjoy her treat before Rosa came to her room with her meds.

After a light knock on the door, she opened it a crack and called out, "It's Harley, Mrs. Neeley. May I come in?"

"Of course, dear," the sweet old lady said. "I always enjoy your visits."

Harley popped inside, excitement building about sneaking the treat to her kind friend. "I know you've already had dinner, but I've brought something I think you'll really like. But it's our secret. Can you keep a secret?" She placed the small bowl on the bed table, scooted it in front of Mrs. Neeley, then gently curled the elderly lady's stiff, arthritic fingers around the spoon.

"Harley—a secret? But why? And you know I'm not much hungry these days. Nothing tastes good anymore." Mrs. Neeley stared down at the bowl, her hand shaking as she hovered the spoon over the sherbet.

"Just try one bite. For me. Please? Just one? I promise it's not the usual tasteless glop from your diet." Harley glanced back at the door that she'd left barely cracked open. Rosa would be here soon. She was three rooms up and very efficient when it came to handing out the pills.

With a resigned sigh, Mrs. Neeley barely dipped the tip of the spoon into the melting orange dessert. After touching it to her tongue, she licked her lips and stared up at Harley in amazement.

"Why Harley, that tastes mighty fine." She dipped the spoon into the sherbet again, took a bigger bite, and was soon shoveling it into her mouth as fast as she could eat it.

"What's going on in here?" Rosa stood at the door with Mrs. Neeley's chart and the small paper cup of meds.

"You just leave her alone!" Mrs. Neeley flourished the spoon like a weapon while motioning for Harley to stay close.

"What have you got there, Mrs. Neeley?" Rosa arched a brow at Harley as she sauntered toward the bed. She made a show of rubbing her nose to hide her smile.

Mrs. Neeley curled an arm around the empty plastic bowl as though attempting to hide it.

"I have an empty bowl here. Must've forgotten to put it on my lunch tray before Harley picked it up." The elderly lady smiled, her eyes sparkling with the innocent lie. She winked at Harley and slid the spoon underneath her bedspread.

"I'll take it for you, Mrs. Neeley, and here, let me straighten your sheets." Harley couldn't resist smiling as she recovered the spoon from the bedclothes, then patted the sweet lady's shoulder.

"See if you can get me more of that fine ice cream," Mrs. Neeley whispered as Harley adjusted the pillow behind her.

"I'll do my best," Harley whispered back.

Rosa followed Harley out of the room and fell in step beside her. "What did you feed that little old lady?"

"Your granddaughter's last sherbet popsicle. By the way, you need to get some more." With a wink and a grin at the kindly nurse, Harley grabbed her jacket off the hook and waved as she headed out the door.

THE RIVER'S gentle expanse of ripples, nudged along by the balmy night breeze, glistened like silver, like liquid mercury beneath the caress of the moon. Harley wriggled her bare toes in the soft clumpy grass of the riverbank as the mighty Mississippi lapped at the shore. A deep inhale treated her to the soothing scents of the river—not the brininess of the sea but an earthy, primordial fragrance teeming with life. Skipjacks broke the surface, making Harley smile. Silly fish tempted by the sparkle of the moonlight and the hopes of snacking on water bugs. She loved living at the river's edge. Her camper wasn't much, but it was hers, and her job at the nursing home enabled her to live on her own. She'd found out the hard way that she couldn't depend on anyone but herself.

A heavy sigh worked its way free of her. Now that it was summer, maybe she should get a second job. That way, she wouldn't have as much time like this. Time to muddle over what could have been—what almost was. If she had a second job, she'd be so exhausted by the time she got home that she'd drop into a deep, dreamless sleep as soon as she ate her sandwich for supper. She slowly nodded as she tossed a pebble into the water. Yes. A second job would not only keep her too busy to think, but it would also grow her savings at a faster rate. Money wasn't the problem, though. Too much time on her hands was the bait that made her inner demons come to life and rip through her heart and soul. A second job might just do the trick. She should definitely look into that.

When she was at work, surrounded by all those sweet, cantankerous old people, she was fine. Her demons stayed asleep and buried deep in the darkness of her memories—right where they belonged. But when she left, when things got too quiet, that was when it happened. When it all came crashing in. All the memories and the cruel game of *if only*. Alone time was a dangerous trigger that brought all her poor decisions back to life.

If only she'd never met Scott, never trusted Scott, and, most importantly, never agreed to marry Scott. If only she'd never walked into that back room at church on her wedding day to find her friend

Sue on her knees in front of him with his pants down around his ankles. Those damn *if only*'s would stab you in the heart every time.

She stiffened her back, sitting up straighter as she pulled in another deep breath and kept her gaze locked on the water. "If only I could float downstream to the ocean and never come back. Be as free as a piece of driftwood on a rolling wave—now that would solve all my problems."

As she scooted closer to the water's edge, the rhythmic lapping of the water against the shore eased the tension in her shoulders and calmed the churning in her gut. The ebb and flow of the tides urged her to come along and play. The distant magic of the ocean called to her, slyly working its way up the mighty Mississippi and whispering to her on the shores of her Kentucky home.

Harley studied the moon as she lay back on the bank just out of reach of the lively waves. "Maybe I could build a raft and float out to sea never to be seen again. Drift off to a magical, faraway land where the love of my life awaits—a love who would never betray me or make me feel like a naive fool."

She waited for the crickets and cicadas to comment on her plan to change her life. Unfortunately, she spoke neither cricket nor cicada and couldn't benefit from their advice even though the grasses and trees almost vibrated with the sheer intensity of their songs.

With a snort at her own silliness, she shook herself free of her melancholy. Self-pity never got anyone anywhere. Time to buck up and get on with it. She dragged herself to her feet and meandered down the moonlit beach. After finding a piece of driftwood, she crouched and poked holes in the sand just to watch as the water filled them in faster than she could dig them.

Tired of the childish game, she stood and stared down at the driftwood, marveling at its intricate knots and whirls making patterns with no beginnings and no ends. "I wish there was someone out there for me. A good someone. Someone kind and loving." She smiled down at the stick. "Find him for me. Okay?" Then she gave it a quick kiss and tossed the piece of wood as far out into the water as she could. She watched it bob and swirl, keeping her gaze locked on it until it floated out of sight. Then she climbed up the riverbank to her lonely bed.

~

"Harley? What kind of name is Harley for a girl?" asked the old man in a rude, growly loudness that echoed across the community room.

"You leave our Harley alone, or I'll unhook the call light for your bedpan!" Frail Mr. Thomas shook his fist at the shriveled man Harley pushed along in the wheelchair. Mr. Jenkins was the newest member of the senior citizen's home, and she hoped to find him a few new friends in the sunny dayroom.

"Now Mr. Thomas, let's be nice. Mr. Jenkins doesn't know the story behind my name, and I don't mind telling it again." Harley positioned Mr. Jenkins beside the bay windows overlooking the pond where the geese were currently swimming with this year's goslings. After locking down his wheels, she tucked the blanket around his frail knees to ensure he didn't catch a chill.

She pulled up a chair beside him, straddled it with her long legs, and propped her chin on its back to prepare to tell the tale she had told many times, but the elders never seemed to tire of it. "You see, Mr. Jenkins. My parents were married for many, many years before I was born. So many years that they decided they would never have children."

As Harley continued the story, she couldn't help but smile as she remembered the devotion her parents had always had, and still had, for each other. "They were so convinced they would never be able to have children that they bought a pair of Harley Davidson motorcycles and hit the open road. But apparently, the open road was exactly what they needed. Because after their first big run, my mother found out she was pregnant with me. Hence, my name—Harley."

Mr. Jenkins peered at her through glasses so thick that the lenses distorted his eyes. "Well, that's the damnedest thing I believe I have ever heard."

With a heartfelt wink, she solemnly nodded and made an *x* on her chest. "Cross my heart and hope to die. It's the truth."

"Well, just where are these parents now?" Mr. Jenkins scowled at her, making it apparent that he wasn't about to be outdone, and was determined that she realized how miserable her life was—simply because of her odd name.

"Last time I talked with them, they were in South Dakota. I'm not sure where they are now. Once I grew up and moved out, they got the bikes back out of storage and hit the open road again." She smiled at the poor old guy, feeling more than a little sorry for him. He was so miserable, he was determined everyone else should be miserable as well.

"So, they deserted you." He shook his head and swayed from side to side in his seat. "I know how that feels. You can't count on anyone but yourself." He seemed to curl into himself, sinking lower in the wheelchair and staring down at his hands in his lap.

Her heart ached for the unhappy little man. She wished she knew of a way to help him battle the cruel reality of growing old and being tossed aside. She scooted her chair closer and gently scooped one of his hands into hers.

"What did you use to do for a living, Mr. Jenkins? Before you came to live here. Tell me about yourself."

His eyes narrowed as he slowly lifted his head. He jutted his sharp chin to a defiant angle. "Don't placate me, girl. Just go away. Don't you have a bedpan to empty or someone's wrinkled old ass to wipe? There have to be all kinds of things you need to do other than sit here with me."

She leaned closer until her nose almost touched his and met his hardened glare with one of her own. "Mr. Jenkins, all I *have* to do is live until I die. Now, start talking."

CHAPTER 3

The wind barely kissed the water's surface, tipping the sapphire waves with lacy white frothiness. Sails in full swell and clear skies across the horizon brought smiles and relief to every man's face. Ronan enjoyed being tossed about by a storm, but he could always count on his first mate, Dagun, to remind him of the many times the sea had refused to return the kinsmen it swallowed. He pulled in a deep inhale of the air's brine, filling his lungs with the lifeblood of the oceans—his lifeblood as ordained by the goddesses.

Dagun's stare burned into him, relentless as the cutting rays of the sun during the Caribbean's hottest season. The squint to his first mate's sharp eyes was a sure sign that he was about to say something Ronan preferred not to hear. But best get it over with. Dagun had never been silent before and wasn't apt to start now.

"Out with it, man," Ronan said. "Better to have yer thoughts out in the open. Be they good or ill."

Dagun cocked his head and continued studying him as if he were an oddity they had drawn up from the depths of the sea. "I can tell something's been troubling ye of late."

This was not the first time the first mate had started a conversation in such a manner, but Ronan had always diverted the man's attention to another subject. But today, he was too weary and distracted by his mother's summons to attempt to sway him. "Taken to reading auras, have ye? Since when do ye possess such talents?"

Dagun idly scratched the stubble darkening his chin. "A mite surly today, are we? Dinna blame me for yer mam calling ye home." He sidled closer and leaned against the wood railing beside Ronan. "Do ye ken why she summoned ye? Surely, she canna fear the season's storms. She understands better than most that ye are at yer safest when ye're in the arms of yer beloved sea."

Ronan shrugged off the question with the gnawing impatience that followed him every waking hour of late. He raked his gaze across the horizon, searching for the elusive answer in the wispy clouds skimming across the skyline. "Who can say what stirred her to call me home? Perhaps she foresaw an event we need to avoid. With Mother, 'tis difficult to know and safer not to guess at it."

Lightly tapping his thumbs together, Dagun stared down at the wide beam of wood fashioned to form the secure railing around the sides of the ship. He ran his hand along the grain smoothed first by craftsmen and then by the forces of nature. Ronan sensed the man was struggling to choose the proper words that would trick him into confessing his soul.

"Perhaps she has seen whatever it is that seems to be troubling ye of late," Dagun said. "Mayhap, she intends to offer her help."

Ronan slowly shook his head as he pulled his focus from the horizon and fixed it on his first mate. "Ye canna stand it, can ye? It's driving ye mad that ye canna work out what might be wrong. Ye are as bad as ye were that time we made port in Dela Ruga, and ye couldna discover whether or not I'd bedded the governor's daughter."

Dagun folded his arms across his chest as he turned and leaned back against the side of the ship. "Well, I beg yer pardon, ye surly git. Forgive me for being fool enough to care about my captain. The man whose life I just happened to save when he wandered into the wrong pub at the wrong time. The one man bound to the sea but didna ken his arse from a hole in the ground when it came to surviving in port. Far be it from me to force m'self on anyone. From now on, I'll be minding me own business, and ye can do as ye will. Let the devil take ye!"

Ronan stared down at the dancing waves lapping against the side of the boat, trying to hide a grin. He'd gone and hurt the poor beggar's feelings. Dagun could be as tetchy as a sore-tailed mongrel at times. Maybe he should share a bit about the strangeness of late. What harm could it do? "Do ye ever feel as though someone is calling out to ye? That ye are supposed to find them? As if they need yer help and are reaching out with every bit of their soul to make ye hear them?"

"Mother of God! I thought ye were safe from the MacKay curse since ye were the second of the three sons to come out of yer mother's womb?" Dagun's eyes went wide, and he backed up a step.

"No, man. I dinna see how it could be the MacKay curse. I've had no dreams about a woman destined to be my mate. 'Tis nothing like Father said he went through when he discovered Mother was fated to be his wife."

Dagun arched his brows nearly to his dark hairline and shook a finger in Ronan's face. "Ye had best be thankful for that small favor. The clan still talks of how miserable yer father was during that time."

"Knowing Father, if he was miserable—so was everyone else." Ronan shook his head again. "'Tis nothing like a dream of a beautiful lass that I'm about to bed but canna touch. I feel a pull toward somewhere unknown. Or toward something—or someone. There is a great sadness reaching out to me. But I dinna ken where it's from or who I am meant to help." Ronan worried with the bronze medallions hanging around his neck.

"Well then, mayhap yer mother can be of help to ye. This sounds like something she could use her gifts for to guide ye. Help ye discover what ye are meant to do." Dagun frowned, his clear blue eyes troubled. "I only met her the one time. Beautiful woman, but I didna miss how the entire clan treated her like a powerful being—a goddess, even—one they didna care to cross."

"Aye." Ronan resettled his forearms on the railing. "Her gifts are oft more of a curse than a blessing. No matter her kindness, her ability to heal and ease pain separates her from everyone. They fear her."

Dagun nodded. "Aye. I remember ye saying the clan was not so accepting of a strange woman from the future. Especially with her abilities and powers."

Ronan straightened, remembering the tale his father had told him many times. "They made her feel so unwelcome at first that she left for another realm for a while, right before the birth of me and my brothers. The Goddess Brid sent her back to Father right as the pains started coming to bring us into the world. Father made her swear to never leave him ever again."

"They accept her now, though," Dagun said. "Albeit with a bit of leeriness." He winked at Ronan. "Ye canna blame them for being a mite careful around her. Ye told me yerself that any time anyone threatened yer da, yer brothers, or yer sister, that those doing the threatening somehow ceased to exist."

Ronan snorted in amusement. "Aye, and no one's ever had the nerve to ask what become of them, either." He pushed away from the railing. "I dinna ken what to tell her, or even if I will tell her anything at all." He aimed a hard glare at Dagun. "If she gets wind of this, there'll be no peace for as long as we are at the dock. Do you understand what I am telling ye, man?"

Dagun backed away, hands lifted in submission. "I'll not be the one to tell the lady a word about her son's melancholy. But if I had a sack full of coins to wager, I'd be betting she'll know as soon as she sets eyes on ye."

"Aye...well, that's why we're taking the long way back to Scotland. I figure I can stall her for about another three weeks. But after that, she'd best be seeing our sails on the horizon." Ronan scrubbed the stubble of his close clipped beard as he turned to take refuge in his quarters.

"By the way..." Dagun followed close on his heels, stealing furtive glances up and down the deck as he lowered his voice. "Did ye bed the Governor's daughter?"

CHAPTER 4

"He's a new one," Rosa said. "Refuses to leave his room—and his bed. It takes tall talking and firm nudging to get him to shift over to the chair long enough so I can change his linens." The nurse shook her head, her expression one of worried frustration as she nodded at the room at the end of the hall.

"What's his name?" Harley eyed the room with interest. She loved a challenge and refused to let the elderly residents give up on her watch.

"Mr. MacCallen. Showed up here with a suitcase full of books about the sea and the clothes on his back." Rosa pulled a cloth shopping bag from her shoulder and handed it to Harley. "I picked him up a change of clothes and some toiletries with money from the general fund. Kind of odd that he had enough money for a private room but only had the one set of clothes with him." She shrugged. "He must be one of those who thinks as long as he covers his behind the one day, it doesn't matter if he has a fresh set of drawers for the next."

"Any family?" Harley pawed through the tote, checking Rosa's choices for the mysterious new resident.

"Far as I can tell, none. Poor fellow didn't even list an emergency contact. He refuses to answer questions about friends or family, just stares out the window until you give up and leave him alone." Her lips thinned into a grim line of determination as she patted Harley on the back. "You know as well as I do that if we don't snap him out of it, he won't be with us very long."

Harley started toward the room. "I know. I hate it when they give up and die of hopelessness." She quietly rapped on the door, waiting a polite few seconds before entering the room. "Good Morning Mr. MacCallen. My name is Harley, and I'm here to help you settle in."

The stone-faced old man lay curled on his side, blindly staring out the window. His bent frame took up the entire bed. In his prime, he must have been a huge man. His shoulder length hair was a glorious, almost sparkling white that only a lucky few inherited rather than the more common yellowish gray of advanced years. His beard was also snowy white, making Harley think that Mr. MacCallen would make a great Santa Claus if he had the round belly to go with the rest of the traditional features.

She rounded the bed so she could look him in the eyes as she pulled his purchases out of the bag. Out of the corner of her eye, she spotted a book with the most vivid pictures of the ocean lying open on the bedside table. Setting aside the tote of new clothes, she reverently picked up the book and poured over the pages. "What a wonderful book. These are the best photographs I've ever seen. Look at the rich blues and greens of the ocean."

"Do ye like the sea?"

The deep rumbling voice startled her, nearly causing her to drop the book. She glanced up from the pages and found herself staring into the most vivid pair of blue eyes she had ever seen—be the person young or old. She smiled and nodded while slowly turning the pages. Care had to be taken so as not to send the old man retreating into his silence.

"Someday," she told him, "I am going to the ocean. Maybe even sail around for a few weeks just to enjoy it. I've always loved the sound of waves, and if the rivers and lakes give me chills, I can only imagine what the sea will do."

"Be careful about waiting for someday, lass. Afore ye know it, all the somedays of yer life will be gone."

Slowly pushing himself up to the edge of the bed, Mr. MacCallen pulled another book out of the drawer. "This one shows the mighty ships that once rode upon the waves." He seemed to be sizing her up, watching her closely from beneath his snowy white brows. His eyes narrowed into calculating slits.

She stifled the urge to toss the book aside and run. What was wrong with her? He was a harmless old man. She opened the newest book he offered and studied its pages. "These look like the pirate ships that are always in the movies. I wonder what it would be like to sail on one of them? Do you think you could spend your life on a ship that size?" She perched on the edge of the chair and turned the book toward him so he could see the pages.

"Aye, lass, ye could spend a lifetime on the open waves if ye had a ship such as that one." He stretched and slowly turned the page, then tapped the next photo with a shaking finger. "This here's where the captain's quarters would be. See what a fine balcony was built so he would always have a view of the horizon?"

Harley leaned over the book. As she studied the picture, she almost swore she could hear the gulls crying out across the salty breeze. She closed her eyes and inhaled deeply, imagining the wind's kiss against her face, the sun warming her skin, and the waves splashing against the ship's creaking hull.

"Ye must go to the sea, lass. I can tell by the look on yer face that ye are one of us."

Harley opened her eyes and grinned, determined to humor the man even though she found something about him quite unsettling. "One of us, Mr. MacCallen?"

He didn't take her question well. Just frowned and shook his head as he sagged back onto the bed. "Never mind, lass. Ignore the rumblings of a tired old man."

Immediately sorry she had squelched his enthusiasm; Harley gently closed the book and studied his weary face. Maybe if he talked more about the sea, he would perk up again. "Did you spend yer life on the sea?" she asked him. "Tell me about yourself, Mr. MacCallen. Tell me about before you came to Pleasant Oaks."

"Some other time, lass. Leave me be now. I am tired." He turned his back to her and covered his eyes with his arm as he curled over onto his side.

Harley drew the light blanket up over his shoulders and tucked it around him. There was more to Mr. MacCallen than met the eye. It was almost palpable, as though some sort of energy pulsated out from him. He was an enigma sent for her to solve.

"That's fine, Mr. MacCallen. Have yourself a nice nap. Later this afternoon, I'll pop back in. We'll get you out of that bed and wander around the place a bit. It's not good for you to hole up in this room all the time."

MacCallen ignored her. He remained silent with his arm over his eyes. She could tell by the rise and fall of his chest that he'd heard her and wasn't asleep. She'd worked in the senior facility long enough to recognize she was politely being dismissed.

She glanced back at him one last time before closing the door. With a determined nod, she concluded that Mr. MacCallen would be her greatest challenge yet.

CHAPTER 5

As soon as he heard the door click shut, MacCallen eased over and peered out from under his arm to make sure he was alone. With the vigor and agility of a much younger man, he sat up and shoved his pillow behind his back while reaching into his shirt pocket. After one more cautious glance at the door, he opened his fist, smiling as he gently caressed the glowing stone in the center of the ancient locket covered in runes and the elaborate knotwork of old.

"Finally. I have found her," he whispered to the precious thing. He carefully pried it open and blew across the interior, which glowed like a silvery puddle of mercury. "She is the one. Did ye see how she took to the books we chose?"

The locket came to life, warming and emitting a softly pulsing light that grew stronger by the moment. A voice as soothing as a gentle summer breeze and musical as a trickling stream rose from the swirling surface of the locket's interior. "Aye, she loves the sea even though she has never touched the waves. I saw the longing in her golden eyes. Is she the one whose loneliness we heard?"

"The only way for us to know for certain is for me to spend time with her. And to do that, I will have to leave this room and be among the others." MacCallen glanced out the window.

Harley wheeled one of the residents out into the yard, laughing and chatting as she tended to the aging mortal in the wheelchair.

He shook his head and blew out a heavy breath. She had to be the one. Not only did she love the sea, but she possessed more compassion than most mortals he had come across over the centuries. "I will have to go out there. Act like one of them."

The locket fretted at this news, its soft light changing from a silvery blue to a troubled red. "Ye must be careful. Ye know I canna hold this glamour long."

"Aye, but with my help ye can. Trust my powers to strengthen ye in this struggle. If I am but among them for a short while, we should be all right." MacCallen nodded his certainty about the matter as he made himself more comfortable among the pillows.

"Goddess Clíodhna will help us too. She has promised us as much." The aura surrounding the ornate locket shifted back to a peaceful, pale blue.

MacCallen shook his head at the locket. "She will demand a tall price from ye—a boon ye will regret. Never has the sea goddess helped anyone willingly unless there be something in it for her. Ye must choose yer words carefully, lest ye regret the pact ye make."

"We understand each other, she and I," the voice said. "Dinna worry about what is being done." The light from the locket flickered, as though growing weaker. "I must go. Make haste, for we have little time. He will soon be home."

Closing the rich, golden halves of the precious piece of jewelry until they clicked in place, MacCallen wound the heavy linked chain around the locket and tucked it back inside his pocket. He slid out of bed and moved to the chair beside the window to watch Harley and plan his next moves carefully. He had been charged with a duty where there was much at stake, but there was also a great deal to win if he managed everything to his liking. Failure was something he never did, and he was not about start now.

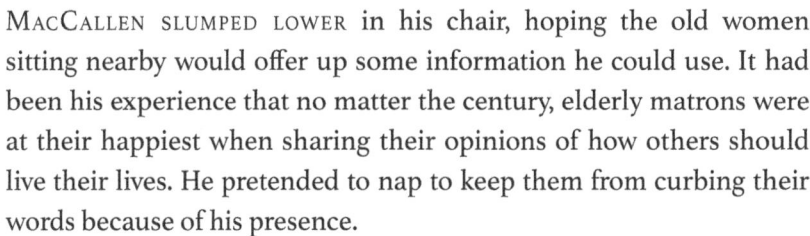

MacCallen slumped lower in his chair, hoping the old women sitting nearby would offer up some information he could use. It had been his experience that no matter the century, elderly matrons were at their happiest when sharing their opinions of how others should live their lives. He pretended to nap to keep them from curbing their words because of his presence.

"That man was an idiot," the one known as Mrs. Neeley said. "A complete, two-timing fool. Who in their right mind would toss aside a woman like our Harley?" She shook an arthritic finger at her friends while peering around the common room as if planning an escape from the retirement home.

MacCallen did his best not to smile and kept his eyes opened to the narrowest slits to watch them but still appear asleep.

"I heard she caught him with his pants down around his ankles with another woman. Is that true?" The tiniest of the women, the one called Mrs. Thorpe leaned forward in her wheelchair, her oversized glasses sliding down her long nose.

"All true—and on her wedding day no less! Can you imagine how that poor girl must've felt?" The heftiest of the trio, Mistress Olive Johnson scooted to the edge of the couch while reaching for her cup of tea.

"And now she doesn't trust any man. Why—I even tried fixing her up with my youngest son, Gerald, but she said she'd rather get a puppy. Said she could trust a dog's loyalty." Mrs. Thorpe shook her head, then pushed her glasses back up her nose.

"Your Gerald is nearly sixty years old," Mrs. Neeley said. "What would a young girl like Harley want with him?" She sat back in her chair, scowling as she folded her hands in her lap.

"Well, at least she wouldn't be alone anymore." Mrs. Thorpe gave a disgruntled snort, picked up her tea, and settled deeper into the pillows stuffed in her wheelchair. "I caught her when she didn't know I was watching. I've seen the loneliness pouring like a flood out of those golden cat eyes of hers."

MacCallen angled the tilt of his head to better take in every word the women uttered. Their nattering proved that the Harley lass was the one. Why else would Fate provide him with so much information about her and her history with men?

"Matilda, I wish there was something we could do for the poor dear. You know how fond I am of her." Olive reached over and patted Mrs. Thorpe's hand. "But fixing her up with your son is not the answer. That child needs a young man who'll stir her blood."

MacCallen dragged his hand across his mouth to cover his smile. *If they only knew,* he thought to himself, then stirred and sat up straighter as Harley appeared in the hallway and headed toward him.

"Are you ready to go outside? It's a beautiful day. Why don't we take a stroll, and you can tell me more seafaring tales?" She held out her hand to help him up while tipping her head at the double doors that opened out into the gardens.

"Thank ye, but no, lass. I think I'd best go back to my room. Been up quite a while now. Weary to the bone, I am." He pulled himself up out of the chair and leaned heavily against his three-legged cane.

"Not even just one lap around the gardens? I promise we'll take it slow." She treated him to one of her beguiling smiles while gently but firmly trying to steer him toward the garden doors.

"No, lass. Not today. Besides, I believe I've told ye every tale I know." He pulled his arm free and ambled down the hall toward his room.

Aggravated that their newest resident appeared to be immune to her charms, Harley chewed her lower lip as she watched him turn into his room and close the door behind him. Mr. MacCallen was a puzzle she was determined to solve. It wasn't good for him to isolate himself the way he did. By the strength of his grasp, she didn't believe his weariness excuse for a minute.

"Harley, come over here and sit with us a bit. Leave that stodgy old Scot to himself." Olive patted the cushion on the couch beside her and nodded for Harley to sit.

"What are you ladies up to? You look like you've been plotting." Harley gave the trio her sternest look, knowing it wouldn't work because they were incorrigible. Every one of them looked like a teenager who'd been caught out after curfew.

"We've decided that we're going to help you find someone. You know—fix you up." Matilda Thorpe smiled so widely that the bright pink gums of her dentures showed.

Alarm bells making the hairs on the back of her neck stand on end, Harley backed away. "Sorry ladies, but I need to check on the dinner menus and make sure we have all the supplies we need." She turned on her heel and nearly ran down the corridor, safely out of range of the plotting matchmakers. The last thing she needed in her life was a man.

"MR. MACCALLEN, ARE YOU FEELING OKAY?" Harley eased open the door, concerned at the lack of response to her knocking. "Rosa said you didn't eat a bite of the pie I snuck onto your tray." The darkened room and silence concerned her. More than once, she had been the one to discover when a person had passed away. "Mr. MacCallen, are you awake?" She held her breath as she eased across the room, hoping for the best.

"Aye, lass. I am awake. Just resting." He shifted positions on the bed, turning toward her.

"Are you all right?" She hurried to the bedside, switched on the softer light over the head of his bed, and gently took hold of his wrist to check his pulse. Slow, steady, and strong. Her heart went out to the poor old soul. Some never adjusted to losing their independence, to life in the retirement home. Some fought it tooth and nail until they died. "What's wrong, Mr. MacCallen? How I can help you? Make life here better for you?"

"Sit with me a while, lass. Here on the side of the bed. Let me tell ye my favorite story about the sea." He patted a spot on the heavy plaid blanket he had brought with him and kept tossed across the bedclothes provided by the facility.

She perched on the edge of the bed, trying not to shake him.

Something about him was not right. His color was off no matter what his heart rate told her. "I thought you said you didn't have any more sea stories? Were you fibbing to me?"

"Hold out yer hand," he said with such a weak raspiness that she contemplated pulling the alarm cord hanging beside the bed.

But something about the mysterious shadows in his eyes stopped her. It was almost a pleading look, like a stray animal begging for scraps and a little kindness. She held out her hand and waited. As soon as he took it between both of his, an eerie tingling swept through her as if she had just shoved a metal fork into a light socket. She forced herself not to jump or yank her hand away. Even though it had been quite a jolt, it couldn't be anything more than static electricity. When he released her hand, a heavy locket, the most gorgeous piece of jewelry she had ever seen, was resting in her palm.

"Mr. MacCallen—how beautiful. Did you find this on one of yer voyages? Was it sunken treasure once?" She slowly turned it in her hand, admiring the exquisite workmanship of the piece. Made of what appeared to be heavy gold, the locket was covered in ancient runes and Celtic knotwork, then edged with curls and cusps of metalwork made to look like the waves of the sea lapping around its perimeter. Each link of the heavy gold chain was also decorated with wavelike lines. The face of the locket had a huge moonstone encrusted in its center. As it warmed to her touch, the gemstone glowed brighter. She couldn't remember when she'd last seen such a lovely piece of jewelry. The necklace mesmerized her, hypnotizing her with its rare, unique beauty.

"The Sea God Manannán Mac Lir fashioned this locket for the Goddess Clíodhna. That stone only glows for those who harbor a true love of the sea and for those blessed few, great magic lies within it." He smiled at her, the brilliant blue of his eyes somehow seeming brighter.

She arched a brow as she held the necklace up by the chain. "Magic, you say?" Sometimes old folks returned to their childhood beliefs, and she would do nothing to take that joy away from them. "Wouldn't that be something?" What kind of magic? Does it grant wishes or teleport the bearer to another place or time?"

The old man's eyes danced as he pushed himself higher in the bed and leaned toward her. "Legend says if ye hold the locket to yer heart and hold yer deepest desires firm in yer mind, they will come true."

"My deepest desires? My goodness. That's a pretty tall order for such a lovely locket to pull off." She stood and smiled at the gorgeous necklace one last time before returning it to the old Scot.

He gave her a lopsided grin and folded her fingers tightly around it while staring deeply into her eyes. "Try it, lass. Where's the harm? Hold it to yer heart. See what wondrous things come to a true believer."

Something about Mr. MacCallen's expression, the strange light in his eyes, made it hard for Harley to breathe—as if the air in the room had gone thick with an eerie uneasiness. She tried to back away only to discover that she couldn't pull free of the old man's powerful grasp. Determined to remain calm, she tried harder to yank her hands free. "It is lovely, Mr. MacCallen. But I need to be going. Let's put the necklace away and get you settled for the night. Okay?"

The aged Scot rose from the bed with amazing ease, transforming from a weak, arthritic old man into a tall, muscular, impossibility with pure determination shouting from his very being. He moved to stand in front of Harley while keeping her hands locked in his. "It is time, lass. I have come in answer to yer call. It is time for ye to go to the one who needs ye as badly as ye need him." He spun her around and yanked her back against his broad chest while keeping her hands trapped between his.

"This cannot be happening." She should have run as soon as he somehow went from weak and old to young and strong. Panic mounting, she tried to wriggle free. "Enough is enough. Let me go or I'll scream, and Rosa will smack you down like you've never been smacked down before."

His mouth near her ear, MacCallen pressed the locket against her chest and whispered, "Close yer eyes, lass. What is yer fondest wish

—yer deepest desire? What have ye called out for all those nights beside the river?"

Harley tried to elbow her way free, but he only tightened his arms around her. She tried to scream, but it came out as a pitiful whisper. The frail old man was long gone, leaving in his place a person impossible for her to escape.

"Who are you?" she weakly rasped. Her heartbeat thundered up into her throat, and her blood roared in her ears.

"Yer guide, lass. I have come to show ye the way. Dinna be afraid. I bring ye no harm." He pressed the locket harder against her chest. The large moonstone dug into her breastbone as if trying to burrow its way into her heart.

Stricken with a nauseating dizziness, Harley tried to scream again, but no sound at all came from her this time. The locket hummed against her, branding her with a strange heat that turned her fears to hysteria. She tried to thrash her head from side to side but found herself unable to move. A searing flash of light blinded her, and a bone-chilling roar deafened her.

I am dying, she thought as the light disappeared and spun her into the suffocatingly silent darkness.

MacCallen smiled down at the locket in his hand. The moonstone glowed with a fiercely bright light. He held it to his ear, and his smile stretched wider at the quiet echo of Harley's pounding heart inside.

CHAPTER 6

"There to the west! Those sails—are they Ronan's?" Aveline stood on tiptoe and pointed over the protective stone walls surrounding the guard's walkway that ran the perimeter of Castle MacKay.

Shielding his eyes from the sun's glare, her father, Laird Caelan MacKay squinted in that direction. "Aye, that be yer brother. I can just make out his colors." He dropped his hand away from his eyes and patted her shoulder as the ship cut through the waters, growing ever larger and more magnificent the closer it drew to MacKay Bay.

"Lucky for the lad we spotted him. Yer mother was about to pull him through the Mirrors if he didna show himself soon." Caelan chuckled. "Ye shouldha heard her ranting about thoughtless males and their inconsiderate ways."

"Aye, Mama has warned me many times about the thoughtlessness of males." Aveline grinned at her father. "She always speaks well of ye, though, Papa."

He snorted. "Dinna be telling lies to yer papa, my fine wee lass. Ye are not too old to be sent to yer rooms without yer supper."

She ignored her father's ability to see through her flattery and turned the conversation back to her brother. "Ronan has been gone too long this time. 'Tis bad enough he leaves us at all. But when he stays away this long, he is hiding something. I just know it and so does Mama. We must help him. Take care of this *thing* troubling his heart before it is too late." A worried edginess filled her as she tried to stretch higher to get a better view over the walls. She loved all her brothers, but Ronan had always been her favorite. She was tired of missing her seafaring brother and fretting about his safety. Just because he held dominion over the seas and everything in them didn't mean he couldn't be harmed. Her brother was still very much a mortal and could die. A deep breath and the knowledge that things would be different now made her feel better. If all worked out as she planned, there would be no need to worry about him sailing away ever again. As the ship skimmed into the bay and dropped anchor, she gave it a curt nod. *Ye will never carry Ronan into danger ever again.*

She noticed her father's troubled gaze tickling across her like a butterfly flitting in her face. When he smoothed her wind-tossed hair out of her eyes, she knew he was about to question her. She had once overheard Mama telling Papa that even though she was the youngest and also a girl, she would still be the most powerful in the mystical ways. Mama had stressed the need to guide her down the right path and teach her to use her gifts wisely. Papa's reply had been filled with leeriness.

But she *did* use her gifts wisely. Or at least, she tried. She wished Mama and Papa would see things her way sometimes. A heavy sigh huffed free of her. They would understand this time. She had done things exactly right and left nothing to chance. Might as well have it out. She turned to her father. "What, Papa?"

"What have ye seen, Avie? Or more precisely, what have ye done?" He eyed her with the sort of stern glare that had always made her squirm—but not this time.

She swept aside the tendrils of her reddish blonde hair tugged loose by the persistent breeze. "I have seen nothing, and why would ye think I have done anything?" She hated hiding that she'd worked with the Mirrors of Time alone, but they had left her no choice. She twitched a shrug, hoping to reassure her father. "I worry about

Ronan. He was gone longer this time." She shrugged again. "Maybe I miss him more than usual because I am older, and he has always understood me better than my other brothers."

Caelan narrowed his eyes at her, clearly unconvinced that she was as innocent as she wished him to believe. "I would bet a keg of ale that ye are up to something, ye wee minx. Save us all a bit of trouble and confess yer sins afore ye commit them, aye?"

"Papa!" She used the same injured tone that always worked on her brothers, but Papa was not so easily swayed. "I am simply glad that my favorite brother is home."

"Did I not hear ye tell Faolan he was yer favorite this past Sunday? And was Latharn not sworn to be yer favorite just yesterday?"

"My favorite is whoever has angered me the least at the moment," she said while attempting a lofty yet somehow worldly innocence. When telling a lie, it was always best to build it upon a kernel of truth.

Caelan scrubbed his face with one hand as if admitting defeat. "Fetch yer mother. We shall go down to the docks together to greet yer brother."

"Aye, Papa." Aveline couldn't resist a smile as she spun about and hurried away.

"Amergin's beard, lass! Slow yerself." Old Emrys, the druid of the clans, hugged the wall of the stairs as she bounced past him.

"Ronan's home!" she sang out as if that excused anything she might do, including knocking the ancient wise man down the steps.

"What mischief is that one into now?" Emrys asked as he leaned against his twisted staff and hobbled over to Caelan.

Caelan shook his head. "I dinna ken, but she bears watching. Ye ken as well as I what Rachel said about her powers. Have ye noticed anything missing from yer library?"

"Nothing. All I know for certain is that I am too old to keep up with a lass more gifted in the ways than any of the druids I have ever known." He stroked his long gray beard with his knobby, arthritic fingers. "I survived training the lads. Faolan, Ronan, and Latharn were nothing compared to that one. She is wilier, more powerful, and also more headstrong than any of her brothers."

"Rachel noticed Avie seemed more intent on learning to control the Mirrors than concentrating on her other studies. Have ye spoken to Faolan or Latharn about her?"

Emrys snorted as he leaned upon his staff. "Ye ken as well as I that those two are useless when it comes to finding out what that wee rascal is up to. She has all her brothers eating out of her hand and not a one of them would be the first to betray her."

Caelan glanced behind them and saw Rachel and Aveline approaching. "I shall speak to the lads. Convince them that as Avie gets more powerful, concealing her mischief might not be the wisest course to take."

∽

"RONAN, THIS WINE IS SUPERB." Rachel narrowed her eyes at her son, studying him over the rim of her glass. She didn't like the gaunt angles of his face. Even though he was still her hulking, broad-shouldered son, he had turned into a leaner, tougher version of himself during this last, lengthy voyage at sea. He had lost the softness of a carefree youth and become a hardened, muscular man who silently commanded respect and more than likely a little leeriness and outright fear.

The shadowy stubble of a day's growth of beard darkened his angular face, lending an even more dangerous look to his handsome features. His thick, dark hair had grown well past his shoulders. He wore it pulled back from his face in braids threaded with leather ties and a gold coin or two.

"He has become a pirate," she said under her breath. Perhaps that was what troubled him. She peered closer, reaching out with her senses. No. It was not piracy that disturbed his inner peace. What was it then? His deep green eyes were fraught with the shadows of—something. She couldn't pin it down and didn't like it one bit. Aveline was right. Something serious troubled Ronan.

She took another sip and offered him a belated smile. "Where did you find this lovely wine?"

"Dela Ruga," he said, returning her smile with one that didn't quite reach his eyes. "I thought you might enjoy it." He shifted uneasily in his seat and glanced around the table as though in search of allies.

Rachel glanced at his plate, noting his food was barely touched. His brothers had not only cleaned their plates but refilled them more than once.

"Father and I looked over the rest of the cargo. Ye did well, little brother." Faolan gave Ronan's shoulder an affectionate shake.

"Did ye see the silks I brought ye, Avie?" Ronan leaned forward and looked down the table at his little sister.

"I did, brother, and I thank ye. But all ye truly needed to bring me was yerself. Ye were gone overlong this time. I feared ye lost to us forever." She shook a finger at him. "I ken well enough yer love for the sea, but ye are still mortal. Dinna worry us like that anymore, ye ken?"

"Now, Avie," Ronan said in a placating tone that Rachel recognized as one that would anger his little sister rather than calm her, "ye know the sea goddess watches over me and keeps me safe."

"Ye were gone longer than usual this time, son," Caelan said. "Ye need to remember ye have family here on Scotland's shores. We watch for yer return and worry about ye during the seasons beset with storms." He shoved his untouched plate away, took hold of Rachel's hand, and held it tightly, making her heart ache for the worry she felt coursing through her husband.

Dagun cleared his throat and thumped the haft of his knife on the long dinner table in the center of the family's private hall. "We had such a prosperous year, it didna seem as if we had been out to sea that very long. Time passes ye by with great haste when the Fates smile upon ye."

"Aye." Ronan nodded, set his goblet on the table, then frowned down at the crimson wine. "Forgive me for causing all of ye worry.

Time escapes me when I am at sea because that is where I truly feel at home."

"This is yer home. Not that ship or the sea!" Aveline fisted her hands on either side of her plate and pinned him with a narrow-eyed glare.

"Aveline." Rachel reached over and rested a hand atop her daughter's. "Be thankful when your brother is among us and be watchful when he is at sea." She rose from her seat, shoving the heavy mahogany chair back with the sheer strength of her concern for her son. "Ronan, I would see you in my solar. Now." She waited for him to rise and follow.

"Mother..." He stared down at his plate, then blew out a heavy groan. "I—"

"Now, Ronan." She stepped off the dais, then looked back and arched a brow at him, waiting for him to find the good sense to follow and not defy her.

"I shall pray for ye," Dagun said quietly as Ronan slowly rose from his seat.

"He'll need it," Latharn said. "She's been storming about the castle for weeks because of his wandering."

Thunder rumbled in the distance. "You had all best pray for yourselves as well," Rachel told them. "Since I have yet to lose my hearing, and do not find your comments the least bit amusing."

"May the goddess be with you, son," Caelan said with a grim nod as lightning flashed and thunder crashed louder.

Rachel didn't attempt to calm herself to control her stirring of the elements and avoid the storm. Her son would do well to remember her powers.

"Just bury me at sea," Ronan muttered as he rose from his chair and obediently fell in step behind her.

∼

RONAN ROLLED his shoulders as he followed his mother down the torch lit hallway to her private solar. This was not only ridiculous but damned embarrassing. He was ashamed to dread a meeting with his mother as much as he did this one. But as a woman descended from a long line of witches, as a woman from the faraway future, Mother wielded unspeakable powers and was not afraid to use them on anyone she deemed deserving of a wee reminder to treat her with respect. He was powerful too but couldn't hold a candle to her—especially when her ire was stirred, and apparently, he had stirred it well.

She stood at the window, framed by the roiling black clouds laced with dancing tendrils of lightning beyond the ledge. Not bothering to turn from her study of the cauldron of thunderheads, she said, "What is wrong, Ronan? Tell me, so I can help you."

He widened his stance and clasped his hands behind his back. This reminded him of the time he had been sentenced to hang for piracy and had yet to figure out his escape. The grim sense of doom was the same. "I dinna ken what ye speak of, Mother. I merely stayed out longer than usual this time."

Lightning splintered the sky and deafening thunder immediately followed. The air crackled with the stinging bite of the storm's energy.

"Don't you dare try to dance around the truth with me. It didn't work when you were a child, and it won't work now." She turned from the window, her amethyst eyes flashing. "You know very well I'm not referring to the time you were at sea. If anyone knows you belong there, it is me. I won't say I like it, but I understand it."

As soon as he opened his mouth, she cut him off with the sharp glare that he and his brothers had always known better than to test. "Think long and hard before you attempt a poorly crafted lie. I know you've been blocking the Mirrors to prevent Aveline from seeing you. She and I both know you're troubled over—something. I even spoke with the Goddess Clíodhna." Her disgusted snort flared her delicate nostrils. "That was a waste of time. Now, tell me what is going on with you before I send you outside to cut a switch for me to use on yer backside."

"We are not back in yer Kentucky, Mother. I am far too old for such a useless scolding." Ronan powered his own show of lightning, farther to the west of his mother's and rising up from the sea.

A powerful crash of lightning hit so close; the air stank of sulfur. The castle walls trembled with the force of the blast as thunder exploded, then rolled across the keep as though determined to level it. "You would do well to think twice before battling with me. Where do you think you got yer powers?" His mother's voice had taken on a lethal tone, clearly warning she would tolerate no level of disrespect.

Ronan bowed his head. "Forgive me. Ye ken I would never disrespect ye—not ever. But I am a man grown and canna be sheltered by ye forever." The tightness in his chest ached even harder. It was almost as if the strange pain needed him to bare his soul to her as much as she yearned to hear it. But he could not. He was far too old to run to his mother as he had done as a child whenever he was hurt or frightened.

Her head tilting slightly to one side, she released a heavy sigh as she studied him. "Your father says I worry too much. But as long as you live and breathe, you will always be my little boy." She moved closer and gently lifted his face, forcing him to look her in the eyes. "Let me help you. Tell me what it is that's clouding those beautiful green eyes." She touched his chest and frowned. "You are hurting, Ronan. I feel it."

He covered her hand with his and slowly shook his head. "I dinna ken what it is," he whispered. "I fear someone has cursed me with some unknown thing that is meant to rip my heart in two. How can ye help with that?"

"Tell me what you feel. Exactly. Maybe if I read your eyes while I listen, I'll be able to hear what it is and discover what's eluding you." She locked gazes with him, willing him to open his heart and soul and allow her to peer within.

The aching throbbed harder, begging him to accept her help. Of course, if he couldn't trust his mother, who could he trust? He swallowed hard and shook his head again. "I hear an eerie call. A tremendous sorrow. There is a great loneliness out there beseeching me to find it—and help it. But I dinna ken where it is, who it is, or how to help relieve their suffering." A restlessness churned deep in his gut as he unburdened his soul. "Someone needs me, Mother, but I canna find them."

Her brows knotting into a worried frown, she eased back a step. "Do you still feel it here? When you're ashore?"

He gave over to a heavy sigh and nodded. "Aye. 'Tis even stronger since we reached Scotland. The closer we drew to home, the stronger the feeling became."

She slowly paced around the room, thoughtfully tapping her chin. "You should be safe from the MacKay curse. As firstborn, Faolan should be the only one to suffer with that." Her scowl tightened, became more puzzled. "Do you know of anyone who might have cursed you?"

"Nay. I've not angered anyone powerful enough to inflict such a misery upon me." He fidgeted in place, ashamed that he'd been unable to solve this problem without her help. "Now, ye ken why I stayed out so long this time, and why I blocked the Mirrors of Time to prevent Avie from visiting with me overmuch while I was at sea. I dinna ken if whatever this is might be a danger to the clan." He clenched his fists so tightly that his knuckles popped. "I canna stay here long, Mother. I'll not risk bringing harm upon those I cherish more than life itself."

"That is not the answer to this, and you know it." She jabbed the air, pointing at him with a sternness that he remembered well. "You should have come to me immediately. We are more powerful together."

He scrubbed a hand across the stubble of his jaw. "Then tell me the answer. Who am I supposed to help—and how?"

Tapping her chin once again, she returned to her pacing. "I don't know. But I will! Give me a little time."

∾

The cloaked figure stood in the cave's mouth, waiting with a flickering torch held high. The steady pounding of the waves echoed and rumbled up through the maze of caverns lining the rocky shore, sending their song back across the sea.

In her favorite form of a powerful wave, the Goddess Clíodhna rose to meet the figure, the white foam on the water's crest rising high in the moonlit night. As the water receded, she stepped onto the stone ledge in the shapely form of a mortal woman. Her white hair glistened in the full moon's light as it poured around her shoulders and swirled down around her feet.

"Ye ken I demand payment for my favors, do ye not?" she said to the hooded figure in front of her.

"I gave ye my oath, and it remains as I stated it before. In return for yer aid, ye will never be forgotten throughout eternity."

The goddess frowned, still unsure if this alliance was a wise one. She narrowed her eyes as she handed over a small sack cinched tightly with a leather cord. "Powerful words for a mere mortal. What do ye know of eternity?"

"I know more of it than ye might think."

With a slight nod, Clíodhna turned and faced her beloved sea. "If yer oath be broken, ye will be the one to replace that soul, ye ken? Manannán grows fond of that heartbeat tickling against his chest."

The hooded figure turned to go, pausing only long enough to say, "I promise, and I never break my oaths."

CHAPTER 7

Ronan threw his plaid around his shoulders and quietly left his room. He couldn't sleep. Whether because the castle failed to rock and gently sway like his ship or because the uneasiness that had plagued him for months now seemed stronger and more unnerving than ever before. He scrubbed his knuckles up and down his breastbone, half wishing he could reach inside his chest and rip the unsettling thing out of his body.

He moved quietly down the dimly lit hallway, pausing to peer out an arrow slit facing the sea. With his face pressed to the tall, narrow opening, he sucked in a deep breath of the briny air and held it. Thankfully, the faithful waters always provided what little ease there was to be found since that unknown force had started haunting his every waking hour.

After descending the stairs, he stepped out into the clan's gathering hall.

His father stepped from the shadows and blocked his way, sending a jolt through him that almost made him draw his sword.

"'Tis unwise to startle an armed man, Father."

"Where are ye off to in the dead of night, son?"

"To my ship. There is no sleep for me here." Ronan glanced around at the multiple clansmen rolled in their plaids and seeking their dreams on the floor.

"Yer mother is doing her best to help. She's in her workroom still, searching every wee book and scroll she possesses." His father fell in step beside him, joining him as he went outside and strode across the bailey. "She will find an answer. She always does."

"I dinna see how she can." This was the first time Ronan had ever doubted his mother's capabilities. "This accursed feeling has haunted me for months now. While I know my powers are not as strong as hers, they are not weak, and yet, they have proven useless in solving this riddle and finding whoever pleads for my help." He pulled himself up onto his great black stallion's back. The horse pawed at the cobblestones, tossed its head, and snorted. It was almost as though the animal sensed its master's uneasiness and was eager to outrun it.

"Dinna underestimate yer mother's powers," his father said. "She is as tenacious and unrelenting as yer sea. Especially when it comes to those she loves. She'll not be at peace until she finds the answer ye seek."

Ronan's mouth tightened with his gritted teeth as he gripped the reins and gazed out into the moonlit night. "The call grows stronger with each passing day. If we canna find the sorrow's source, I fear I shall go mad with it and never know peace again."

His father nodded. "It sounds much like the madness I experienced before I found yer mother and made her my wife. Dinna despair, lad. She will find the answer. Ye ken the way she has with the powers."

Ronan didn't wish to hurt his father by shrugging off his advice, but the man couldn't possibly understand the maddening frustration of hearing a cry for help and not knowing who it was or from whence it came. While some thought him a coarse man hardened by the sea, he couldn't abide the thought of someone trapped or suffering simply because he was too thick-skulled to discover their whereabouts. He tipped a nod back at the keep. "Go to yer bed, Father. I willna sail off into the night if that is what ye fear."

His father grinned. "'Tis doubtful ye could get past the magical wards yer mother placed at the mouth of the bay. But ye are always free to try."

∼

RONAN HANDED off his horse to the clansman guarding the docks and hurried up the gangplank to his ship. The fathomless depths of MacKay Bay from mouth to the shore enabled even the largest ships to dock rather than have to drop anchor and come in by skiff. As the gentle swell of the waters welcomed him and moved the deck beneath his feet, the tension knotting his shoulders eased, and his burdens seemed lighter. Aye, this was where he belonged—on the water and breathing in the tang of the sea.

He paused on deck and stared up at the stars that had led him on many journeys. When out on the open water, the sky, and the sea were almost as one—vast and alive with mysteries they shared with a chosen few. His ship spoke to him, quietly creaking and groaning as the calm waters gently tugged at it, whispering to come and play, come and find another adventure. Ronan ran his hand along the railing, stroking it with pride and affection. "Not yet, old friend. We must visit with family for a while and make our apologies for neglecting those who love us."

After one last glance at the open waters beyond the mouth of the bay, he headed aft and pushed into his cabin, tossing his plaid across a chair. The wall of windows that hemmed in the berth, his enormous feather bed, one of the few extravagances he indulged in, welcomed him with a view of the moonlight dancing across the rippling waters.

He stretched and rolled his shoulders one last time before collapsing on the bed and giving himself over to the comfort that felt like home. A jaw-cracking yawn reminded him of his weariness and urged him to fold his hands behind his head and sleep. The effortless motion of the ship made his eyelids heavy. Just as he relented and closed them, an eerie thumping, urgent and close, demanded he remain alert and give it his attention.

Ronan propped up on one elbow and squinted around the moonlit room, scanning it for anything out of the ordinary. The insistent sound continued, taunting him to find it. With his head cocked to one side, he leaned forward and concentrated on the soft, steady thumping that had come to sound more like a heartbeat the longer he listened to it. "Where the devil are ye?" he whispered into the shadowy darkness.

He slid out of bed and prowled around the large cabin that would make any captain proud. The urgent pounding led him to a small leather pouch tucked in with his logbooks on the built-in shelves behind his desk. He gingerly picked it up, holding his breath as the thumping pounded faster and louder. After unwrapping the leather cord cinched around the neck of the bag, he eased it open and peered inside. A faint light filled the tiny pouch, but it wasn't bright enough to reveal the contents. Ronan upended the bag over his palm, then blew out an irritated snort at the sight of the Goddess Clíodhna's locket. "What in Brid's name are ye playing at this time, Clíodhna?"

The large moonstone set in the locket's cover glowed bright with a lively, blue-white light. The piece trembled in his hand, vibrating with the steady rhythm of the trapped heart or imprisoned spirit within it. "Damn ye, Clíodhna," he growled soft and low.

Long ago, the sea goddess had been known to trap unwary men's souls, but he thought she had finally set that cruel habit aside after Brid imprisoned her for several centuries for that crime against mortal man. As he closed his fingers around the ancient piece of jewelry, the familiar yet mysterious ache in his chest stirred as though his heart needed to beat in sync with the heartbeat of the lost soul trapped inside the golden case.

With it clutched in his hand, he stormed out of his quarters and charged his way to the ship's bow. Facing the open sea, he held the locket up to the moonlight and shook it. The necklace's chain snaked down his forearm, wrapping around it and squeezing as if begging for his help.

"Clíodhna!" he roared into the wind while scanning the cresting waves for any sign of the goddess. She never ignored his call. But as minutes passed and nothing happened, anger filled him. She needed to heed his call. Only Clíodhna could answer the riddle to the mystery in his hand.

"Clíodhna! Come to me now!" He leaned over the railing, glaring down at the waves lapping against the side of the ship. Still no answer —no sign at all. The longer he waited, the more he realized the sea goddess had chosen to ignore him for the first time in his life.

He straightened and leaned back against the railing, slowly turning the locket, studying it from every possible angle. The energy trapped inside quietly implored him to set it free, and it feared he would ignore it. The moonstone's glow flickered in time with the beat of the imprisoned heart.

"Mother will know." After retrieving the leather pouch he had discarded in his quarters, Ronan placed the locket back inside and tucked it inside the cloth sash tied around his waist. The heartbeat tickled against his flesh, its constant begging to be free pulling at his heart. He loped down the gangplank.

"My horse!" he called to the guard at the end of the dock.

The man hurried to untie the beast and bring it forward.

Ronan leapt upon it and rode hard back to the keep, reining in the beast in the outer bailey and dismounting. He didn't bother tying it off before charging up the steps. The only thing that mattered was the mysterious locket, and the heartbeat trapped within. He strode across the great hall, stormed into the back archway, and vaulted up the steps to the upper level two at a time, shouting down the passage as he neared his mother's workroom, "Mother! Mother!" He didn't care if he roused the entire castle.

The workroom door flew open, revealing his harried mother, her eyes wide with alarm. She charged into the hallway and met him.

"What is it? What's wrong? I thought you'd gone back to your ship to rest."

"I did and was nearly asleep when *this* demanded my attention." He pulled the pouch from the sash around his waist and thrust it into his mother's hands.

After raking her disheveled hair behind her ears, she carefully drew the necklace out from the pouch. She squinted at the piece, studying it just as closely as he had. With a worried frown, she held it aloft by the chain and tilted her head, watching it as it slowly turned. The moonstone glowed brighter, its eerie light creating a flickering aura around the piece.

"Where did this come from?" His mother sounded as though she were in a daze, her voice low and reverent as she cradled the locket in her hands.

"It was on my shelves with my logbooks. That belongs to the Goddess Clíodhna—the one she used to imprison souls before the Goddess Brid convinced her otherwise. I have seen it before. Clíodhna once showed it to me while telling me of her legends." He slowly circled his mother as she pressed the golden locket to her chest.

Mother closed her eyes, a studious frown puckering her brow as she tilted her head to one side and appeared to listen to something only she could hear. With a startled jerk, her eyes flew open. She hurried to return the ornament to its pouch, cinch the bag tightly shut, and knot the leather ties. "Did you call to the sea goddess?"

"Aye. Twice. Even used my powers to strengthen the call." Mother's reaction worried him. Something he couldn't quite identify flickered in her eyes.

"What did she tell you once she finally appeared?" She set the pouch on the table in the center of the room, shaking her head at Ronan's father as he entered with his sword drawn and held between his hands as though ready to cleave the thing in two.

"She ignored me. Didna even send so much as a breeze to flutter my sails." Ronan raked a hand through his hair while keeping his focus locked on the leather pouch quietly thumping on the table.

"What does it mean, Rachel?" Father circled the pouch with a wariness that betrayed his need to destroy the thing with whatever means it took.

His mother caught her bottom lip between her teeth and nervously chewed it. "The pull of loneliness and sorrow plaguing our Ronan comes from that locket. I don't know who is trapped within, but their soul cries to be free."

Ronan drew his dagger, cut the leather ties from the pouch, and dumped the cursed bit of jewelry back into his hand. With a hesitancy born of knowing the sea goddess's powers, he risked touching the moonstone on its cover. "Why would Clíodhna trap a soul? Surely, she knew the Goddess Brid would imprison her again for doing such?"

His mother dragged a weary hand across her eyes, then massaged her temples as she lowered herself into a chair beside the table. "I don't have that answer, son. I do know she's a temperamental one, as changing as the sea itself—and wants no one to believe she fears Brid as much as she does. I also worry that this might be some sort of trap. Perhaps, she used her powers to imprison evil inside that tiny tomb this time."

"Nay, Mother." Ronan shook his head and thumped his fist to his chest. "If it was evil, I would feel it. A knowing about this thing has settled deep within me. Loneliness, great sadness, and the desire to be free lie within that wee prison. There is something familiar about that soul, as well." He shook his head. "I canna explain it, but I know what I know." He held the locket against his chest, determined to listen to it with his heart this time rather than his head. The longer he held it to his heart, the brighter the moonstone glowed.

"Ronan, stop!" His mother snatched the necklace out of his hands, shoved it back inside the pouch, and returned it to the center of the table. "We must go carefully before we choose a course of action. I also want to hear Emrys's thoughts."

"Your mother is right," his father said as he caught hold of him by the shoulders. His grip tightened and Ronan struggled to free himself and retrieve the bag from the table. "Whatever is in that locket has been there for some time. One more night of waiting to be freed willna hurt it."

Ronan stared down at the small pouch. It seemed so lost and forlorn in the center of the table. He could almost hear the soul sobbing—and it sounded like a frightened woman. He swallowed hard and fisted his hands to keep from snatching it up and cradling it close. His parents were correct. They had to take great care with this. One more night of loneliness for that poor soul, and himself too, was a small price to pay if it meant they might solve the mystery tomorrow.

He moved closer to the table and leaned over it, drawing his face close to the locket. "I am here," he whispered. "Take heart. I willna desert ye. Soon, ye shall be free."

The moonstone glowed brighter, then the rhythm of the thumping slowed to a calmer beat.

"Never lose hope," Ronan told it. "Never."

THE SIGHT of her troubled son in the clan's main gathering room made Rachel shake her head. When she had finally convinced him to delay any action until she talked with Emrys, she'd thought he'd take refuge in his old rooms to get some rest. Instead, he had gone down to the great hall, sat at one of the long trestle tables, and pillowed his head on his arms.

Half the night, she had lain awake, listening to the eerie heartbeat trapped inside that locket. Why had Ronan found himself in possession of the sea goddess's infamous trap for unwary mortals? And why had the fickle Clíodhna ignored her son's call? The wily goddess had always come to him. The first time he called her, she showed up as a curious sea lion. Ronan had been a mere six months old at the time, and Clíodhna had harkened to his every call since.

Rachel held tight to the pouch as she climbed the steep stone stairs to Emrys's library. Perhaps the old druid was awake by now and might be able to shed some light on this dangerous mystery in their midst.

"Daren't ye bring that infernal thing in here! Accursed thing kept me awake all night, and I am too old for such nonsense!" Emrys kept the door open no wider than an inch, his bloodshot eye peering at her through the crack.

"Open this door! Our Ronan needs us, and I cannot believe you're refusing to help him." She leaned hard against the barrier, determined that he let her in. "I know there has to be something in that massive library of yours that could help him."

"Druidic lore passes from master to apprentice by rote. We put nothing to the page," he said while struggling to hold the door shut despite her shoving it.

"Do not stand in there and lie to me, old man. You came to my century and saw the power of the written word. I know you've been recording everything you could recall ever since." She bumped the door with her hip. "How can you be so strong, you withered old dog? Open this door!"

"My strength comes from my connection to the earth," he said with a growling grunt. "Just because ye are a twenty-first century witch doesna mean ye know everything nor possess the ability to overpower me."

"Something has to be in your books. I've already checked mine and found nothing. Let me search through yours. I will not have my son endangered by some foolish whim stirred by that hard to get along with sea goddess."

"The boy must do this alone. I have seen it. Now, get that thing away from me." Emrys stumbled away from the door, brandishing his staff as though trying to protect himself from an evil curse.

"What have you seen? Tell me." Rachel stalked toward him, waving the pouch at him like a weapon.

"I have seen a potential future, ye ken? One best avoided, if ye ask me. If anyone but Ronan breaks the wee curse upon that locket, then their soul will be sucked inside to replace the soul already there. Whoever worked the spellwork on that necklace knew exactly what they wanted—and that was for Ronan to be the one to open it." Emrys shielded his face with his arm, peeking at the locket, then hurrying to turn his gaze away from it.

"You are certain of this? You have seen it?" Rachel debated whether to trust the old wizard. Their relationship and trust in one another had never been on solid ground. "What of Ronan's soul when he opens it? Did you see that likely future as well?" Fear made her heart pound as she envisioned her son trapped inside that golden case.

"All I could see of that future was that Ronan appeared relieved—and then a mite confused. But rest easy, Rachel. Those golden walls will not imprison him. My vision told me that the Goddess Clíodhna forbade it. Ye ken how much she loves him." Emrys sagged down onto his cot, struggling to keep his eyes shielded from the thing within the leather pouch.

"I hate this. You know how volatile she can be. The sea goddess is like a spoiled child when she doesn't get her way." Rachel sank into a nearby chair, the long night taking its toll on her energy as well.

"Aye, but Brid favors yerself and yer children. Clíodhna willna challenge the Mother Goddess, and as I said, ye ken how much she loves Ronan." Emrys curled onto his side and rested his staff across his body for protection.

Rachel shook her head. "It is her love for Ronan that worries me."

~

RONAN ENTERED his mother's private solar and found her staring out the window that overlooked the sea. The waves crashed against the base of the cliff that made the MacKay fortress even more impenetrable. They called out to him—teasing him to forget his worries and return to where he belonged. The untamable, ever-changing waters would always possess him. Mother still struggled with his destiny to be forever entwined with the sea, and she had never been easy with the Sea Goddess Clíodhna possessing such a fascination with him.

She turned from the window; her usual composure replaced by a worried scowl.

Father stepped forward, a fierce protectiveness in the set of his jaw. He kept one hand on the haft of his sword and the other on the small of Mother's back. He was ready to defend her even though he had never possessed or fully understood the powers she and their children commanded.

Faolan, the firstborn of their powerful trio, shifted in place, eyeing the room with a leeriness and readiness to spring into action. His blonde hair was already shot with strands of silver, reflecting his cautious and protective nature towards his family and the clan he would someday lead.

Latharn, the youngest, his hair as reddish blonde as the sly fox for which he was named, appeared to be the only one at ease with the meeting. Known for his craftiness and quick wit, he had yet to encounter a situation he was unable to manage—which lent to a bit of arrogance on his part. Ronan feared that someday, his little brother would meet his match and regret being so overly self-assured.

And then there was baby sister, Aveline. Ronan noted her nervous fidgeting and the uncertainty in her pale green eyes. She kept darting furtive glances around the room as if expecting—what? He stifled a groan and refrained from shaking his head. That lass was up to something. He could smell it. He only hoped it was nothing they would all end up paying for.

"Ronan." His mother moved toward him with the leather pouch held aloft. "After talking with Emrys and scouring every written source I could find, I think we can help this captured soul." Her dark brows drew together, and she appeared almost tearful. "But we must go with care for if this goes wrong—"

"I understand." He pulled in a deep breath and held out his hand. "Give me the locket, Mother. I need to be the one to do this." He would endanger none of the others. Not when this *thing* had plagued him for weeks before finally coming to rest at his door.

She removed the necklace from the pouch and placed it in his hand. "I am glad you feel that way because it appears you are the one who must release whatever is imprisoned. Emrys has seen it, and I also scried the mists for what we are about to do. You hold the fate of the soul within this golden prison."

He stared down at the locket, mesmerized by the gentle pulsing flicker of light the large, iridescent moonstone emitted. The heartsong beat steady and strong, stirring a protectiveness in his chest, a caring for the tortured soul that had somehow found itself caught in the sea goddess's unholy game.

"How do I break the curse?" he whispered without taking his gaze from the necklace.

"We must surround you with an elemental circle. It will protect you—and us—from being pulled into the sea goddess's prison to replace the soul already there." Mother motioned to his brothers and sister to join hands and gather around him. When his father stepped forward, she shook her head. "No, Caelan, my love. I am sorry. To include you in this circle would endanger you, and I refuse to risk it." Love shone in her eyes as she tipped a nod toward the window. "Stand over there. Please, my love. You should be safe there."

"What of yer safety?" Father growled with nostrils flared like an angry bull. "I will not have ye endangered, wife. That soul can stay imprisoned if it means risking yerself or one of our children."

"We cannot leave that soul trapped, and I promise we will be as safe as possible." Once again, she nodded for him to move over to the window.

Baring his teeth like a cornered animal and emitting a low growl, Father strode over to the window. He drew his sword and held it ready to strike.

Mother turned to Faolan and nodded to her right. "Take the northern point, my son. You will draw down the element of earth."

With his mouth set in a grim line of resolution, Faolan nodded once and moved to where she directed.

"Latharn, take the southern point of our circle. You will be best to draw down the element of fire." With her hands folded in front of her, she resettled her footing as Ronan's youngest brother positioned himself as instructed.

"Aveline, take the east. Call forth the element of air." Mother moved to the side of the circle opposite Ronan's sister and opened her arms. "I will take west—the element of water."

As everyone joined hands, the locket became alarmingly warm. Ronan turned it over in his hand, noting how the moonstone glowed brighter and the gold casing swelled and retracted with every beat of the heart trapped within. "And me, Mother?"

"Your place is in the center. Right where you stand at this moment. You will invoke the most important element of all. You will be spirit." She lifted her hands and linked them with Faolan and Latharn. Aveline did the same.

"Hold the locket to your heart," she told Ronan. "We will each speak in turn, and when the energy has risen, the words will come to you to release the soul. Speak from your heart and soul. Everything you need to help the imprisoned one lies within you." She turned and gave his father a stern shake of her head as he inched closer to the circle. "Please, Caelan. No."

"I dinna like this," he growled.

"It must be this way," she pleaded.

"Father—please." Ronan hated he had brought such dangerous unrest to his family, but it was too late to turn back now. "We will protect Mother. I swear it."

His father locked eyes with him. "And who will protect ye, son? And yer brothers? And yer wee sister?"

"We are more powerful together. Ye ken that, aye?" Ronan kept his gaze locked with his father's, refusing to back down and look away.

His father bared his teeth again, but he returned to his post at the window.

Mother gave a heavy sigh, then nodded for Faolan to begin.

"I invoke the power of the earth spirit. Ground us safely in what we seek." As Faolan turned to their sister and nodded, a deep green aura surrounded him.

"I invoke the power of the air spirit," Aveline said. "Breathe truth into what we seek." As she turned to Latharn, she became illuminated with a glowing aura of white that was so bright it was almost blinding.

"I invoke the power of fire spirit," Latharn said. "Purify us with yer power." Flames licked and swirled around him as he turned and looked at their mother.

"I invoke the power of the water spirit," Rachel said. "Bring us balance and dominion over the seas in what we seek." Aglow with a deep blue aura, her voice echoed with the depths of the mystical energies humming around the circle and passing through them.

With the now white hot locket clutched to his chest, Ronan closed his eyes and threw his head back as the elemental powers surged through him, charging his senses with their powerful energy. In a voice deep and echoing with that power, the words he needed came forth from his heart and soul. "By the strength of my spirit, I release yer bonds and welcome yer soul into my arms. Come and take refuge. I grant ye sanctuary and will keep ye safe from those who bound ye. Never again will ye ever be so accursed."

The locket split in two, exploding with a blinding white energy that swirled and burned, searing his skin and making his hair crackle as though determined to turn him to ash. Ronan held fast as the power unleashed a deafening howl and roared even hotter.

"I will not be consumed," he roared, struggling to hold tight to a shifting form thrashing in his embrace. It had to be the soul. The soul was fighting to be free. "I am here to help ye," he shouted to it. "I will keep ye safe."

The soul writhed, pushed, and shoved, struggling to escape. He felt sure if the thing had teeth, it would have shredded him. "Dinna fear me," he bellowed into the inferno's deafening roar. "Allow me to help ye."

Then silence fell with an abruptness that took Ronan to his knees. The power he had struggled to hold turned into a soft, warm weight that doubled him over. He opened his eyes and stared down at her. For it was a lass, a breathtaking lass with long, silky tresses as black as his own. Her dark lashes fluttered, but her eyes remained closed. Her lips, full and red and holding the promise of the sweetest kisses were barely parted.

A sudden panic took hold of him. Did she live? Or had prying her free of the locket torn her life away? "Dinna be dead," he whispered as he cradled her closer and pressed an ear to her chest.

Her heart beat steady and strong—the same rhythm he had heard within the locket.

"Did she survive?" his mother asked.

"Aye," Ronan said without looking up from the beauty in his arms. "Her heart beats true."

CHAPTER 8

Harley rolled over onto her side and hugged her head. It felt like an over-inflated balloon ready to pop. "Lovely. A sinus headache. What a way to start the day. Thank you, Kentucky humidity and pollen." She massaged her throbbing cheeks and brow bones, then groaned again and squinted her eyes shut even tighter. They burned like she'd spent the night in a smoky bar. The pollen must be super high on the riverbank today. And what day was it? Had the alarm gone off? Was she scheduled to work?

"What is wrong with me? I never wake up this wonky." She shoved herself upright while still holding her head and risked opening an eye.

A strange man sat there; his startling green eyes locked on her in a curious stare.

Throat clenching terror kept her from screaming, but she came to her senses enough to shove both hands under her pillows, searching for the trusty prybar she kept there for security purposes. But her fingers didn't hit the cool metal of the iron bar. It was gone. How could it be gone? She scrambled as far away from the man as she could get and scraped her elbow on the stone wall at her back. Stone wall? What?

She blinked and forced her eyes open wider, flitting glances all around while keeping the stranger firmly in her sight. High ceilings with huge wooden beams supporting them were overhead. Medieval looking tapestries were pulled back from open windows as if they were meant to be curtains. Torches burned in iron holders on the wall. Rough looking candles that definitely hadn't come from the fancy gift shop downtown were sputtering on a nearby table. And come to think of it, the man with the long black hair, sitting in front of her with a build like a weightlifter, wasn't exactly dressed like the average tourist who might wander along the riverbank in front of her camper.

"Where am I?" she asked, her voice broken and raspier than a rusty hinge. She coughed and thumped her chest. What was wrong with her? She cleared her throat and tried again. "Who...who are you, and how did I get here?" A loud hiccup broke free of her, a sure sign that the panic making her heart pound was about to make her puke. Nasty habit she had, tossing her innards whenever frightened out of her wits. "Answer me!" she screamed between erratic hiccups.

"Calm down, lass. Ye are safe now." He rose from the chair and held out his hand.

She jerked away, pressing back against the cold roughness of the wall. "Keep away from me. I might not have my crowbar, but I'm not afraid to fight." Although, from the looks of him, the fight wouldn't last very long. She'd never met a man his size. Tall as...well, she couldn't say exactly how tall he was, but he towered over her and probably had to bend to walk through high doorways. And his shoulders were so broad she couldn't see around him.

"I mean ye no harm, lass," he said quietly, as if she'd hurt his feelings. "As I said, ye are safe here. In my home. Castle MacKay." He gave her the same smile he'd had when she first opened her eyes—a friendly smile. A kindly kind of smile. Concern and kindness appeared to fill those emerald eyes of his too. "My name is Ronan MacKay. What is yer name, lass?"

She chewed on her bottom lip and debated whether or not to tell him. After another glance at her strange surroundings, she decided keeping her name a secret was pretty futile at this point.

"Harley," she whispered.

"Mistress Harley," he repeated with a Scottish brogue that was a little hard to understand because of the way he rolled his *r's*. But his deep voice made up for it. It was the kind of soothing, reverberating sound a person could float away on and listen to in their happiest dreams. "Do ye have a surname, Mistress Harley?"

"A surname?" She knew what he meant, but everything was so strange, so—frightening—for lack of a better word. The world didn't even smell right anymore. The air was filled with wood smoke, grease burning—maybe from those candles—and a general earthiness layered with a clean, crisp fishiness that made her wonder if they were near water. "My surname?" she said again to buy herself more time to sort through this chaos.

"Aye, lass." His dark brows drew closer together and something that might be genuine worry flickered across his striking handsomeness that belonged on the cover of a romance novel. He reached for a pitcher and an impressive antique pewter goblet, poured liquid into it, and handed it to her. "Here, lass. Drink. Ye seem a mite confused."

"Yes." She nodded as she took the cup. "Confused is a very accurate word for me right now." She sniffed the contents before she sipped and frowned. "Why does this smell like alcohol?"

"Alcohol?"

She squinted down into the goblet, then sniffed it again. "Is this beer?"

Mr. MacKay gave her a bewildered shake of his head. "Nay, lass. 'Tis ale. Would ye prefer mead?"

She stared at him for a long moment before answering, unsure exactly what to say. "Uhm...water, maybe? Could I have some water?" Had she been in an accident and had a head injury, maybe? A wreck, perhaps, and a film crew had rescued her and brought her to their set? She shook her head at that. No. That was ridiculous. Nothing like that was going on anywhere near her town. "Where did you say this is? I really need to be getting home, Mr. MacKay."

"Ronan."

"What?"

"Call me *Ronan*, lass, ye ken?"

"I'm not sure what *ken* means." She handed the glass back to him. "Where is this again?"

"Castle MacKay."

"There is no Castle MacKay in Kentucky," she whispered, pressing so tightly back against the wall that the roughness of the stone blocks became almost painful.

He didn't answer. Instead, he went to a cabinet on the far side of the room and poured something from a different pitcher into another glass. When he returned and handed it to her, she couldn't read his expression, and that increased her uneasiness almost more than she could bear.

"Water for ye, lass. 'Twill make ye feel better to wet yer thrapple."

She sniffed it first, her deep inhale echoing in the metal goblet.

Ronan sadly shook his head. "I would never lie to ye, Mistress Harley."

"Just Harley." She took a sip, and it was the sweetest, cleanest water she had ever tasted. And he was right. It made her feel better. "Harley Trent."

He smiled as though grateful for the gift of her full name, but this time the smile was sad and that same sadness was reflected in his eyes.

"I need to get home now," she said, making up her mind to challenge him and find out just how nice and kind this handsome, dark-haired pirate type Highlander really was.

"This is home now, lass. Scotland of 1407." He gave her a compassionate nod. "I am sorry, but I dinna think we can get ye back to wherever or whenever ye once lived. If we did, the sea goddess might attempt to foist more mischief upon ye."

Harley clutched and stretched the neckline of her cotton pullover, finding it difficult to breathe. A trembling she couldn't control shook her so hard, she spilled her water—but didn't care. Spilled water was the least of her worries right now. "I cannot be in Scotland or the year 1407. I live in Kentucky and the year is 2008."

He bowed his head and blew out a heavy sigh that made her want to scream. "I am sorry, lass."

"Stop calling me *lass*! I told you my name is Harley!"

With his mouth clamped shut in a tight, unhappy line, he gave her a quick nod. "Forgive me. I meant no insult." Another heavy sigh gusted free of him as he leaned back in his chair and pinched the bridge of his aquiline nose. "What is the last thing ye remember before ye woke up here? Where were ye? What were ye doing?"

She stared at him, refusing to buy into whatever mind game he was trying to pull. He might be handsome, and he might be kind, but that didn't mean he wasn't dangerous. She shoved the glass of water into his hands, then scooted back out of his reach against the wall. "I don't know. I just woke up, and I was here." She nervously wet her lips. "Tell me where *here* really is. And I want the truth this time."

"I told ye, lass—Harley, I will never lie to ye. This is Scotland. And it is the year 1407."

A sharp knock on the door made her jump and bang her head against the stone wall behind her. "Dammit!" She squinted while rubbing the sting from her skull.

A woman dressed in a costume straight out of a movie about ancient Scotland entered the room. "I see she has awakened."

"Aye." Ronan rose from his chair again and gave a respectful dip of his head. "Mistress Harley Trent, this is my mother, Rachel MacKay—lady of Clan MacKay."

Hugging herself against a renewed wave of hysteria, Harley swallowed hard to keep from vomiting all over the bed. She saw the resemblance between the two. Both had the same dark hair, although the woman's was streaked with silver, and she had the strangest eyes. Not green like Ronan's but a blue so rich and dark that they were purple."

The lady of Clan MacKay approached the bed and gave Harley the sort of look that made it seem as if she understood exactly what

Harley was going through. "You can call me Rachel. Don't be afraid. You'll come to no harm here."

Harley sniffed and swiped a hand across her face, trying to stop an onslaught of tears so she wouldn't start hiccupping again. "You don't sound like him." She sniffed again, grappling with the rising hysteria about to choke her.

Rachel motioned for her son to step back, then sat in the chair beside the bed. "That's because I've only been in Scotland for the past twenty-eight years. The accent isn't quite the same as those who are born to it." She tipped her head to one side and grinned. "What part of Kentucky are you from? You sound like home to me."

"Southwestern tip of the state. By the Mississippi. What do you mean I sound like home?"

Rachel leaned forward as though about to share a juicy secret. "I'm from that part of Kentucky too. From the year 2007. I was probably about your age when I traveled back in time."

"Wait. What?" Harley peered closer at the older woman with the fine lines at the corners of her eyes and the silver in her hair. "That's impossible. If you were my age in 2007, and you've been here twenty-eight years, then how can I be here and be my age, and you be…your age now…when I'm from the year 2008?" She didn't want to insult Ronan's mother, but the facts begged an answer.

Rachel shrugged. "That, I am afraid, is a question for Einstein. I can only tell you what is. Not how the laws of the universe control the outcome."

Harley scrubbed her face with both hands, wishing she had never opened her eyes and discovered herself dumped in the middle of this confusing mess. "How did I get here? I don't remember what I was doing or what was going on before I woke up here. All I know is that when I woke up, I expected to see my messy camper—not the inside of an ancient castle."

Rachel gracefully rose from the chair and rested her hand on Ronan's shoulder. "My son will help you find your answers, and you have my word that our entire family—our clan—will help you in any way we can. I promise you, there's nothing you can tell us that will surprise us. Unless it's about an invention from the future that was introduced after I crossed over into the past."

After an obvious nudge from his mother, Ronan held out his hand. "I will never hurt ye or lie to ye, Harley, and I am verra glad to be the one to help ye."

After a nervous glance at Rachel, Harley pressed a hand to her chest. Her heart was about to pound its way out of her ribcage. "I am so afraid," she whispered, hating to appear cowardly. She had always been brave, never afraid to tackle any adventure, but this—this adventure terrified her.

He eased forward with a gentleness that made her both leery and hopeful that he was as nice as he really seemed. "I willna hurt ye, Harley, and I swear no one else will hurt ye, either. I would never allow that. Come, now. Try to trust me."

She stared at his outstretched hand, then willed herself to find the courage to take it. Warm and callused, something about his touch steadied her. She was still confused and frightened out of her mind, but something about her hand enclosed in his gave her the strength she needed to move forward.

He gently tugged, helping her out of the bed. "Come, lass—I mean, Harley. Time to find yer land legs, and see yer new surroundings. We are quite welcoming here. I promise ye."

"Since it appears to be a Scottish habit, you can call me *lass* if you want to. Sorry about snapping at you before." She held tight to his hand, pulled herself up, and immediately lost her balance and fell against his chest.

He wrapped his arms around her and held her close. "Easy there, lass. I have ye and willna let ye fall."

There was something about his scent—the same wild crispness of the open sea gusting in through the window across the room, mixed with a warm male she instinctively knew would never harm her. She breathed him in while noticing the impressive expanse of hardened muscle pressed against her. "I'm just a little light-headed...sorry." She pushed away and resettled her footing but kept hold of his arm. Her cheeks burned with embarrassment.

Rachel smiled and headed for the door. "Ronan will bring you to the main hall for supper. You need to eat and rebuild your strength. Then we'll find you some clothes, so you'll feel more comfortable about moving among our people and not appearing out of place."

"Not appearing out of place," Harley repeated, staring at the door that Rachel closed behind her. Her heart rate returned to panic mode, and she fixed Ronan with a pleading look. "Please tell me this is just a bad dream—or a terrible joke."

He gave her a sad shake of his head. "It is real, lass. I ken it is a lot to understand, but I promise ye, ye are not alone."

"Why are you being so...nice?" She didn't want to insult him, but why would he bother to help her, bother to be so caring?

"Because I have listened to yer heartsong pleading for my help for several long weeks now, and I am determined to accept the task and do so."

RONAN WAS eager to do anything it took to erase the worry from Harley's beautiful whisky colored eyes and coax her full lips into a smile. Her skittishness as they slowly made their way down the hallway concerned him. She was not ready to meet the others. Not yet. The way she clutched his arm to steady her hesitant steps shot her nervousness into him, made him ache to put her at ease.

"Do ye think yerself strong enough to climb a few steps?" he asked, then changed his mind as she stumbled. It took all his reserve to keep from sweeping her up into his arms. "Would ye mind if I carried ye, lass?"

She pulled away and eyed him with the leeriness of a trapped animal. "I can walk, thank you. For some reason, I'm just a little stiff and shaky, but I'll be fine. I just need a little time to get all the kinks worked out, that's all." She jutted her chin in the direction they had been headed. "You go ahead if you have things to do. I'm sure I can find my way."

"It would be more than a little rude to leave ye." Why would she expect such behavior from him? Never would he stoop to such coarse manners. Such actions would be beyond contemptible. "And nothing I have to do is more important than yerself."

"Why?" She hugged herself as they walked, refusing to hold on to his arm any longer.

"Because—" He didn't have an answer for that. He was used to giving orders, having his word accepted without question, and not having to explain himself. "Because ye *are* important. Let that be the end of that. Would ye like to step outside and breathe in the sea air? It always strengthens me." He gave her an awkward shrug. "It might strengthen ye as well."

She caught her bottom lip between her teeth, cringing with indecisiveness as she glanced first at him, then eyed both directions of the long hallway. "Some time outside might be really nice before I meet everyone else." She seemed to pull into herself, like a cowering animal that had been mistreated in the past. He ached to hold her and assure her he would let no harm come to her.

"Will there be many people at supper?" Pure fear shone in her eyes.

He didn't wish to make her worries worse, but neither would he lie to her. "I dinna ken how many there will be, lass. But it will be more than just Mother and myself. Of that, I am sure."

"Can we get outside without running into a lot of people?"

"Aye." He offered his arm for her to take. "The tower steps are beyond that archway. But I warn ye, they are steep and winding. I can carry ye, if ye wish." The memory of her warm softness in his arms, when the locket had freed her, made him hunger to hold her again.

"No, thank you. I'm pretty sure I can make it." She took his arm, softening the sting of her refusal.

Ronan walked slowly, doubting her belief in her recovery but not wishing to upset her again. "Ye asked if there would be many people at supper. Are ye one who prefers to be alone?"

"I wasn't that way in Kentucky, but I think I'm that way now. Here in this century. Especially the way I'm dressed." She shifted with a deep intake of air, seemed to hold it for a few steps, then let it ease back out. "I don't belong here," she said in a voice so soft he almost missed it. "I'm afraid of what people might do." She halted and gave him a panicked look. "If they think I'm a witch or something, they'll try to burn me at the stake."

He took hold of her shoulders and leaned down to level his gaze with hers. "Ye are safe here at Castle MacKay, lass. I swear it."

"So, I'm trapped here inside this castle forever?"

The desolation and hopelessness in her voice squeezed his heart. He had to help her, make her believe that no harm would come to her —at least, not on his watch. "Do ye know how the sailor ate an entire whale all by himself?"

Her sleek, dark brows knotted over her leery eyes. She stared at him as if he'd gone barmy. "What?"

"The sailor that ate the largest whale in creation—all by himself. Do ye ken how he did it?"

"No," she said, with an impatient roll of her eyes. "How did he eat the whale all by himself?"

"One bite at a time." He waited for her to sink her teeth into the old tale and understand its meaning.

"I don't get it, and I really don't think this is the best time for telling jokes." She scowled at him and flipped her hands in the air. "I'm kind of in the middle of a genuine crisis right now, in case you hadn't noticed."

He couldn't resist reaching out and touching her cheek. "I have noticed, lass. That is why I asked ye about the sailor eating the whale. For ye see, if ye try to live yer life all at once, worrying about how ye will face everything from now until the time ye die, ye will drive yourself mad about things that might not even happen. But if ye refuse to let yer mind run away with ye, and live yer life one day at a time, one moment at a time, ye will find those small *bites* much easier to chew and swallow."

Her knotted brows untangled, and she fixed him with a sheepish glare. "Oh."

He offered his arm again while struggling not to appear smug.

"For now, we are walking down the hallway to the tower where we shall climb the steps and look out across the sea."

"And breathe."

He nodded. "Aye, and breathe in the air's freshness and listen to the terns keening out their woes." He took her hand and ushered her through the stairwell's archway first. The spiral staircase was far too narrow for them to walk abreast. "We shall enjoy that moment and not move on to the next until ye are ready."

"In that case," she said as she climbed in front of him, making her way up the winding stone steps, "I might be the first skeleton up in your tower."

Momentarily distracted by the way her lovely, round arse swayed in front of him, Ronan blinked and silently scolded himself for not paying attention. "Nay, lass. Ye will be fine after a bit. Just ye wait and see." She was finer than fine right now, but he couldn't very well tell her that—not when her trust in him was still so tenuous.

She paused and bowed her head, leaning forward with her hands pressed to the walls as though to wedge herself in place. Even in the tower's torchlight, Ronan could tell her knuckles had gone white from her tight hold on the stone blocks surrounding them.

He surged forward and scooped her up just as she went limp. "Lore a'mighty—ye stubborn lass." He tucked her to his chest as if she were no more than a wee bairn and finished the climb to the circular room at the top of the tower. Rather than lower her to one of the benches along the walls, he sat and held her, cradling her head to his shoulder. "Dinna fash yourself, lass. I have ye," he whispered into her hair as he pressed a kiss to the top of her head. As soon as he had done it, he went still, wondering what had possessed him to do such a thing. But it had seemed so natural—as if he had done that for her a thousand times before.

She barely stirred, curling into herself and nuzzling closer as if needing his warmth to soothe her.

The worrisome ache in his chest, the one he had endured for weeks on end until the locket had appeared; surged hearty and strong once again, but this time, the ache had everything to do with the woman in his arms, and he knew it. He swallowed hard, denying what it might mean. It could not be possible. He was not the firstborn MacKay son. The curse of finding and securing a predestined heartmate belonged to Faolan—not him.

Nay, Harley Trent was his responsibility because he knew best how to battle the games the Sea Goddess Clíodhna put forth for her own amusement. But he couldn't resist bowing his head and breathing in Harley's sweetness. She smelled of flowers. Not the blooms of Scotland, but the fragrant petals of the plumeria from the warm, exotic isles of the West Indies. And she smelled vulnerable—and in need of a guardian.

She shifted again and this time; she pushed against his chest, lifted her head, and stared at him. "Uhm...sorry."

Mesmerized by the way her sooty lashes brought out the golden tawniness of her eyes, Ronan tightened his arms around her. "Ye have the eyes of a jungle cat I once came upon during my travels."

She blinked. "Is that good or bad?"

He couldn't resist a smile. "In yer case, lass, it is lovely as can be."

When she nervously wet her lips, he almost groaned but staunched it before it escaped. "I think I can stand now," she said, then glanced toward the open doorway leading to the outer walkway that encircled the tower. "Walking should be good too."

He helped her stand, rising beside her and holding her arms until satisfied that she wouldn't fall. "I feared the steps would be too much for ye."

She cut him with a hard, side-eyed glare. "I had to try."

"Aye, that ye did." The beauty had some fight to her, and that made him glad. She would need it to adapt to this time. "Come." He gently led her to the walkway, keeping a firm hold on her arm. "Look out upon my precious sea. I have never found a better tonic for what ails me."

The way she parted her lips when her awestruck stare took in the sparkling waters made him ache to kiss her. She leaned forward and rested her hands atop the stone wall as the waves danced and rippled out to the horizon. The breeze caught hold of her long dark hair and lifted it, fluttering her curls out behind her like an angel's wings.

"So beautiful." Her voice echoed with wonder and reverence. She pulled in a deep breath, her delicate nostrils flaring with the effort. And then she smiled, a genuine, relaxed smile, and he knew he was powerless against her. Anything she asked of him, anything she wanted, he would move heaven and earth to give her whatever she desired.

She closed her eyes and lifted her face to the breeze; her smile becoming even more serene. "I always wanted to make it to the ocean someday."

"And now ye have."

She opened her eyes and nodded. "And now I have." Ever so slowly, she meandered along the walkway, running her hand atop the wall as if fearing she might lose her strength again. She kept her gaze locked on the view, as if unable to pull her attention away from the sea. "Are we on the east coast of Scotland? Is this the North Sea?"

"Aye." He pointed at the docks below. "And that is my ship. The Selkie."

"The Selkie," she repeated softly, then leaned forward and rested her cheek atop her arms folded on the wall.

"Harley?" Ronan caught hold of her by the waist.

"I'm fine." But she didn't lift her head, just stared out at the sea.

He moved closer and wrapped an arm around her. "Let me help ye into the tower room. Ye can rest upon one of the benches while I fetch ye more water. I should never have brought ye up here in yer weakened state. Pray forgive me."

"No, this is what I needed." She shifted against him with a deep sigh. "It reminds me of home. How I'd lay on the riverbank and daydream about floating down to the ocean—like a mermaid or something." Her sad smile as she lifted her head made him hurt for her. Her eyes gleamed with unshed tears. "My parents will be so worried when they can't find me."

"And yer husband too, I expect?" It was selfish of him to ask such a thing, but he couldn't stop the words from tumbling out of his mouth.

Her jaw flexed and hardened. "No husband. I dodged that bullet just in time."

Dodged that bullet? He would have to ask Mother about that saying to be certain he understood what Harley meant.

She eased away, putting a disappointing amount of distance between them. "I guess we should go downstairs now. No sense avoiding the inevitable any longer."

Her emotionless tone weighed heavily upon him. Their earlier closeness had disappeared like mist hit by the rising sun. He reached for her, wondering if she would relent and take his hand again. "We shall go then. If ye feel ye are ready."

She stared at his hand so long with such a bleak expression; he readied himself to snatch hold of her in case she tried to throw herself over the wall and be done with Scotland, the year 1407, and him. When she slid her hand into his, he released the breath he hadn't realized he held.

"I'm ready," she said, but her tone implied otherwise.

∼

HARLEY SCRUBBED her hands on her jeans, the nervous sweat dampening her palms making her even more self-conscious. She glanced around the cavernous room before moving to the chair Rachel directed her to with a smile and a nod.

Up on the dais, with a multitude of tables and benches arranged in rows down the center of the room, Harley felt like she was either the main course or the centerpiece being given away as a door prize. At least the other tables were empty. She wondered if Rachel or her husband, the laird, had ordered that done to give her a chance to grow accustomed to her surroundings. She almost snorted at that thought. It was going to take more than an empty room to get her used to the impossible to believe situation she had opened her eyes to just hours ago. *Just hours ago.* So much had changed in but a few hours. She huffed a mirthless laugh at time's cruelty. It felt like she'd been trapped in this craziness for an eternity.

She raked her fingers through her windblown hair, trying to tame it and tuck it behind her ears while wondering if mirrors had been invented yet. Of course, she might be better off not knowing what a mess she looked like.

A loud crackle and pop drew her attention to the impressive fireplaces on opposite sides of the room. They were large enough to hold fully matured trees. A young man, probably in his teen years, tossed massive trunks into the already blazing hearths, handling the monstrous pieces of wood as if they were matchsticks. If Ronan had spent his youth doing such chores, it wasn't any wonder he had the body of a muscular superhero now.

As the boy turned from stoking the fires, he bowed to her, then smiled. She forced a weak smile back at him, then tried to curl into her chair and disappear. She did not belong here. How had she ended up in this place and time? No matter how many times she tried to backtrack and remember, she couldn't recall anything other than waking up in the feather bed upstairs. She remembered her life before this craziness—just couldn't quite seem to locate the one memory that might explain how she came to be here.

She jumped as Ronan took a seat beside her.

"Easy there, lass. 'Tis just me. The food ye are about to eat will help as much as the sea air did. Trust me." He reached as though about to touch her arm, then stopped and rested his fist on the table instead.

She jerked again as three men as tall, muscular, and massive as Ronan entered the room. Each of them arched a brow at him as though communicating without speaking.

"Mistress Harley Trent, these two are my brothers, Faolan and Latharn. We three entered this world just minutes apart. Faolan is the eldest, and Latharn is the youngest."

She noticed Ronan narrowed his eyes at his brothers, glaring at them as if warning them to behave.

"Welcome to our home, Mistress Harley," Faolan said with a

polite bow before shooting a bored scowl at Ronan. "Calm yourself, brother. She has not been in my dreams."

"In his dreams?" Harley repeated to Ronan. "What does he mean by that?"

Before he could answer, Latharn seated himself on her other side. "'Tis good to meet ye, lass. Mayhap ye can tell us of the future?"

"Latharn!"

Latharn rolled his eyes and turned to the older man who had entered the room with them. "Mistress Harley, allow me to introduce ye to Laird Caelan MacKay—our father."

Harley once again caught her bottom lip between her teeth. Now she knew where Ronan and his brothers had gotten their size. Taller than his sons but not quite as muscular, Lairn Caelan MacKay cut a striking figure with his sandy blond hair whitened even more with streaks of silver.

"It's an honor to meet you, Mr. MacKay." Her voice trembled and cracked, no matter how hard she tried to sound braver than she felt.

"*Laird* MacKay, lass, if any of the clan is about. But when it's just family, ye may call me Caelan." He settled a stern glare on his youngest son as he seated himself at the head of the table. "And please, Mistress Harley, it would be best for all concerned, if ye refrained from telling anyone specific details about the future. The tapestry of time is a delicate thing, indeed. The slightest meddling could be disastrous."

"I understand." Or she would when she had time to think about it. Currently, her thoughts were muddled enough, trying to sort out how to adapt to the current dilemma that was her life. She glanced at Latharn and noticed his eyes glinted with mischief. That one was trouble. She'd bet her camper on it. She bit her lip and bowed her head. Her poor little camper. It wasn't much, but it was hers, and now it was gone.

Determined not to cry in front of Ronan's family, she lifted her head and nodded at Caelan. "Don't worry about me meddling with—"

"The tapestry of time," he prompted.

"Yes. The tapestry of time. I don't know any secrets that might change the course of the world."

"You never know," Rachel said as she shook out the cloth beside her plate and placed it in her lap. "Changing the most innocent of details might prevent you from ever existing."

Harley frowned, pondering the possibilities. "Like—if while I'm in the past, I kill one of my ancestors, then I might never be born?"

"Ahh...wise as she is beautiful." An elderly man who epitomized every long-haired, long-bearded wizard Harley had ever seen in the movies hobbled up to the table, leaned his cane against it, then sat in the seat across from her. "I am Emrys, master druid of the clans." He nodded his snowy white head at her, and the tips of his mustache twitched upward in what she assumed was a smile.

"Master druid of the clans?" Harley's mind spun with all the intricacies of the world as she now knew it—or as she didn't know it. Now, she had to make sure she didn't alter history. Wasn't her mere presence here altering history? What about that? Didn't she hear a joke about this once? If you traveled to the past and killed your grandfather, how could you ever be born to travel to the past to kill him? She pressed a hand to her chest, not feeling well at all and praying she wouldn't embarrass herself by getting sick at the table. She didn't even know where to run to if she needed to throw up. No indoor plumbing or a nice, quiet porcelain bathroom in which to hide.

Emrys leaned forward and squinted at her. "Try not to think about it o'er much, lass. 'Twill only make yer head pound."

"Dinna fash yourself, Harley. Soon ye will feel right at home, and I promise to help ye any way I can." A young woman joined them and slid into the vacant chair between Rachel and Caelan.

"Mistress Harley, this is Aveline, our youngest, who often takes her time when it comes to getting to where she is supposed to be." Caelan glared at his daughter, then returned his attention to Harley. "We will all do our best to help ye adjust to being here, and I promise ye the protection of Clan MacKay."

"But ye will soon find that Ronan is yer greatest protector," Aveline said. "After all, 'twas him who freed ye from the locket." She winced and twisted away from her mother as if she had just been kicked under the table.

"Freed me from what?" The hairs on the back of Harley's neck stood on end as she searched everyone's faces for more information. An eerie chill tingled across her, and her stomach churned. "What did you mean by that?"

"Aveline, you will go to my solar and wait," Rachel said through clenched teeth while scowling at her daughter.

"But Mama, she needed to—"

"Now!" Rachel rose, caught Aveline by the arm, and walked her to the archway.

Aveline disappeared into the stairwell but sent her frustrated wail echoing back to them as Rachel returned to the table.

"What did Aveline mean?" Harley asked, determined to get an answer.

Rachel stared at her, clearly not comfortable with the subject. "Are you familiar with any ancient Celtic lore? Tales of the gods and goddesses?"

Harley blinked, confused by the shift in the conversation. "A little. Maybe. I was always more interested in tales about the sea. Mermaids and sea monsters and such."

Ronan interrupted his mother by holding up a hand as he turned to Harley. "Did ye happen to hear any stories of the Sea Goddess Clíodhna?"

"No." She bowed her head and massaged her temples, wondering if information overload was to blame for the sudden vicious throbbing. "The only stories I remember about sea gods or goddesses were always about Poseidon or Calypso. What has that to do with what Aveline said? Explain what she meant that it was you who freed me from a locket." A locket. She squinted and dug her thumbs harder into her temples. What was it about a locket? There was a memory there that she just couldn't quite bring forward.

Ronan gently turned her toward him while bending so he could look her in the eyes. "It seems yer soul was trapped inside the Sea

Goddess Clíodhna's locket until we performed the ritual to have ye released."

"What?" She searched his face for a sign that this was a very poor joke. That couldn't be true. "Gods and goddesses are just stories," she said. "Mythology, rituals, and magic—that's all the stuff of good fiction. Not what happens to an average girl from Kentucky."

"Then how else would ye explain yer presence in fifteenth century Scotland, lass?" Compassion shone in his eyes and echoed in his voice.

She shrugged out of his grasp and stumbled away from the table. "None of this is happening. This is all just a bad dream. All I have to do is wake up, and I'll be back in my camper." That was the only possible explanation for this situation. All she had to do was will herself to wake up.

Ronan eased toward her. "I know this is all hard to believe. Difficult to accept. But ye will fare much better if ye sit and try to listen calmly."

"Calmly? Sit and listen calmly?" Her voice cracked, and she didn't care. She'd earned the right to sound like a shrieking harpy. "I sit and listen calmly to the sermon at church or to the safety training video at work. This..." She flicked a hand at the room at large. "This magical mumbo jumbo is not something I can sit and listen to calmly." She jabbed a finger at him. "I can't listen calmly when my life has been turned upside down, and everything I have ever known or loved is gone!"

As she backed away, she bumped into one of the long trestle benches, swaying as she clutched at it to keep from tumbling to the floor. As Ronan moved closer, she grabbed one of the long handled ladles resting on it and swung it at him. "Stay away from me! No matter what you've said, I don't know who you really are. Not when you only tell me what you want me to hear. Just leave me alone. I don't trust any of you."

"Lass, please." He took another step toward her. "I didna tell ye about the locket, because ye have had so much to take in since ye awakened." He reached for her. "Please, come and sit."

Apparently, he thought her a trusting fool—or puppy in need of obedience training. Fine. She'd show him obedience. She wound up and slung the heavy iron ladle at his head, then turned and charged up the staircase. Outside would have been better, but she wasn't quite sure how to get there. The battlements would have to do. Maybe she could find a low side and shinny down the walls or something. Mama and Papa had always teased and called her monkey when she was little because there was nothing she couldn't climb.

"Harley!"

The panicked roar made her run even faster, pumping every last ounce of adrenaline she possessed through her veins. She had to get away. Hide. Jump. Climb. Something. She didn't care which option it took to take control of this craziness and make it make sense.

CHAPTER 9

Ronan took the steps two and three at a time. He had to catch her before she did herself any harm. The wildness in her eyes before she charged away made him fear she would do whatever it took to escape this time and place. He spotted her as he reached the tower room. "Harley!"

She didn't look back, just scampered down the path along the top of the outer wall. The moon, full and swollen, peeped over the horizon, seeming to rise from its pale reflection shimmering across the waters. Waves steadily crashed below as if shouting for Harley to run faster.

Panic filled him as she threw a leg over the wall and peered downward. "Harley! No!"

The wind whipped her black hair all around. The rising moon illuminated her face, revealing the tears streaking down her cheeks. "Get away from me," she shouted, her voice shaking.

Ronan forced himself to take a step back and keep his arms relaxed at his sides. "Harley," he said softly. "Please—dinna cast away yer precious life."

She glared at him, then held her hair back from her face and peered over the side of the wall again.

"I shouldha told ye about the locket. Forgive me, lass. I was merely trying to shield ye." He yearned to move closer but feared to do so. Her hopelessness, her heartbreaking desperation held him at bay.

She straightened but still straddled the wall. As she stared out at the waves, she slowly shook her head. "I am completely, totally lost this time." She shrugged while still staring out at the sea. "I realize my loneliness in Kentucky was by my own choice. I kind of holed up after the wedding debacle." She flipped a hand at the sea and shook her head again. "But this. Here."

He had no idea what she was talking about, but at least she was talking and not throwing herself down to her death. Ronan eased a step closer.

She pulled her gaze from the sea and locked her eyes with his. "This is—" She thumped the wall. "This is not my fault. I did not do anything to end up here."

"I know it is not yer fault, lass. No one would ever say that." He inched closer until he stood near enough to grab her off the wall should she try to jump. But he didn't touch her. Not yet. Something deep inside told him to let her talk until she grew weary of the sound of her own voice. "Ye willna be alone here, Harley. Not ever. I am here, and here I will stay." A huffing laugh escaped him. "I didna ken I was searching for ye, but now that I've found ye, I'll not be letting ye get away."

She frowned at him and narrowed her eyes. "You don't even know me."

"I know enough."

She swung her leg back around and hopped down from the wall. With her hands tucked into fists, she hugged herself and leaned back against it, then sniffed and swiped the tears off her cheeks. "I will figure out a way to survive here, and with any luck, maybe your mother or that druid of yours can find a way to send me back."

Ronan arched a brow, crossed his arms over his chest, and leaned against the wall beside her. He didn't want her to go back to her time. And no matter what she said, he *did* know her—or at least felt as though he had known her all his life. He tilted his head and studied this very frustrating woman whom he needed in his life, and that alone scared the living shite out of him. "Ye canna go back to yer time."

"We'll see what your mother and the druid say—I don't remember his name, but you know who I mean. Until that time, do not feel compelled to protect me. Just go on about your business—or whatever it is you do." She frowned, as though befuddled, then nodded. "Your ship. That's it. You pointed out your ship. Go back out to sea. I've survived on my own for most of my adult life and done just fine. No one is responsible for me but me. I refuse to be anyone's burden."

"Ye canna survive on yer own, lass. Not here. Not in this time. Unless ye plan on joining a nunnery, ye will soon discover ye need a man to protect ye." And that man would be him—whether she wished it or not.

Her golden eyes sparked like angry embers, and the depth of her scowl would frighten a lesser man. But not him. Her fire made him all the more determined to align with her, protect her, and who knows—if a fair wind blew upon them, even cherish her the way she should be cherished. If she would allow it.

She pushed away from the wall, marched back to the tower room, and yanked the stairwell door open. "Do not underestimate me," she said with a growling feralness before storming out of the room and slamming the door behind her.

"Do not underestimate me either, lass," he warned soft and low. "For that will be yer undoing."

~

Ronan didn't move from the tower room, just glared at the door she had slammed behind her. With his arms crossed over his chest, he scowled at the barrier as if trying to intimidate it into telling him what the devil had happened to the women of the future.

Not only had he offered her the protection of his home, but had also assured the hysterical wee hen that she need not fear anything or ever worry about being alone. What else could she possibly need? He understood it would take her time to adapt and move through her mourning of her home and losing friends and family from the future, but after that, he was here for her. As was his family and clan. She need not worry about anything.

And he wasn't a vain man when it came to women, but he'd never had a shortage of maids eager to warm his bed. Since he was second born, he didn't have to worry that they were merely after the title of laird's wife either. That was Faolan's duty. When a fine, lovely filly sought his company, he knew it was because she hungered for him—not some title that might come to him at some point in time.

With his frequent absences out to sea, he was a mystery women loved to unravel—the fish they longed to land and permanently fix within their homes. Something about trying to tame a man from his wandering ways appeared to make him irresistible.

The door opened, revealing not Harley, but his father wearing a smug expression that warned Ronan he was about to receive some sage advice he'd rather not hear.

"Harley has gone to yer room," Father said, "and locked herself in, it would seem. I dinna think she realizes those chambers are yers."

Ronan turned and stared out at his beloved sea. "I can promise ye the lass doesna ken those rooms are mine. If she did, they would be the last place on earth she would seek refuge."

His father rumbled with an irritating chuckle. "A wise man once told me ye must be patient. Persistent and patient. The lass has much to adapt to. It will take some time." He thumped Ronan on the shoulder. "But trust me, when at last ye win her heart, all will have been worthwhile."

Ronan tore his focus from the sea and eyed his father. "I never said I wished to win her heart. I am merely attempting to help the lass through her loneliness—help her adapt to this time." He wasn't ready to fully divulge his feelings for Harley—not when he barely knew them himself. Best to be cautious about anything he said about the complicated maid.

His father arched a silvery brow. "Ye may be second in line and think yerself safe from the curse, but trust me, son, this lass is the one ye were meant to be joined with. I see it in yer eyes. Hers too, if ye look close enough. Even old Emrys is already wondering when the two of ye shall be wed."

"*Wed?* That old goat has finally lost his mind." Ronan shifted in place, resting his hands on the ledge as he fixed his gaze on the watery horizon. "My life is at sea. I need no wife pining for me when I'm gone or weeping every time I leave."

His father clapped him on the back, then turned to leave. "We dinna always ken what our destinies are until they force us to acknowledge them. Just because ye have always been at home at sea, doesna mean that's where the rest of yer days will be spent."

"Hmph." Ronan locked his focus on the mesmerizing waves crashing against the rocks on the far shore of the bay. He wanted to be with Harley. Protect her and shield her from loneliness, but he was none too sure about marriage. Granted, she was a fine woman and had said she loved the sea as well, but...He rolled his shoulders, trying to shake free all the questions and uncertainties his father had left him with. Marriage. He shuddered. A dangerous word he tried to never utter aloud.

∾

HARLEY PACED BACK and forth across the stone floor covered in heavy rugs woven somewhere other than Scotland. She felt sure of it. They had to have come from Turkey or Iran—no, *Persia*. At least that's what she thought Iran was called in this century. *This century.* Those words made her ready to drop to her knees and sob, but she refused to give in to the urge. She would not cry anymore. Tears solved nothing.

She clutched her aching head and tried to slow her whirling thoughts, which were only contributing to her sense of panic. Time to stop fretting about how she had gotten here and concentrate on how she would either get back or survive here in fifteenth century Scotland.

Her heart hammered harder and faster as she recalled Scotland's bloody history from a class she'd taken years ago. She tried to remember the dates of the worst years but gave up when her mind refused to cooperate. Dropping into a chair beside the hearth, she sagged forward and held her head in her hands. Even in her wildest dreams, she had never imagined life ever becoming this crazy.

She leaned back and allowed herself an exhausted sigh, glancing around the room and fully taking in the decor for the first time since she'd first opened her eyes to this strange new world. An enormous, canopied bed with dark sapphire curtains and counterpane sat off in its own private alcove. When she'd awakened to find herself here, apparently, she'd been on the pillowed bench closer to the hearth. The pillows, coverlets, and cushions on the furniture were all done in vibrant blues that reminded her of the deepest stretches of ocean she'd seen depicted in pictures and photographs.

Intricate tapestries adorned the tall windows, all of them showing sailing ships braving the open sea. Shells and frothing waves decorated the mahogany chair arms and bed posts. Everywhere she looked was a reminder of the sea. Ronan would like this room, she decided, then found that mildly disturbing. If the man loved the sea, and this was his home, had they displaced him to put her up in his room?

A quiet knock on the door interrupted that worry. She scrubbed her face with both hands, wishing she had a sink of cold water to perk her up. "Come in." As soon as she said the words, she wondered if she shouldn't have. How did she know who was on the other side of that door?

Rachel entered with a food tray balanced on her hip. "I know you must be starving. But I thought you'd be more comfortable eating up here—since meeting the family didn't go quite as smoothly as I'd hoped."

Harley hurried to take the tray, set it on the table, and motioned to one of the chairs for Rachel to join her. "Thank you for being so thoughtful. I'm really sorry about before. I don't want to seem ungrateful about you and your family taking me in." She raked a hand back through her hair and perched on the edge of the seat opposite Rachel. "I'm afraid I'm struggling with all this." She gave a weak wave of her hand, encompassing her surroundings.

Her face a picture of grim understanding, Rachel nodded as she poured a ruby liquid into a tankard. She placed it in front of Harley. "Drink up. Mulled wine. It will do you a world of good, and I know my telling you I understand probably doesn't make a difference in how you're feeling. But I really do know what you're feeling right now, and I promise, it will get better."

Harley pulled apart a small loaf of bread and popped the steaming bite into her mouth. The warm yeastiness of the freshly baked bun made her even more homesick. She hurried to wash away the feeling with a deep sip of the spicy wine. "What did Aveline mean? About Ronan being the one destined to help me since he'd released me from that goddess's locket?"

Steepling her fingers under her chin, Rachel narrowed her eyes as she stared at Harley. "Have you ever thought about magic or the mysteries of life that can't seem to be explained?"

Harley paused with another bite of bread halfway to her mouth. "Up until now—no." She shoved the bite into her mouth and scowled all around the room as she chewed. "But now? I think I'm going to have to rethink my current belief system." She shook her head. "I guess you could say my mind has been forcibly changed."

Rachel smiled and poured herself a mug of wine. "A wise decision. And since you said that, I don't mind sharing what Aveline meant by what she said." She settled back in the chair, propped her elbows on the arms, and balanced the mug between her hands. "I am gifted with the ability to connect with the mystical energies. As are my three sons and my daughter. With this ability, we are able to see and do things that others cannot. It was viewing Ronan's destiny to which Aveline referred."

Harley tucked her legs under her and clutched her mug to her chest. "Ronan's destiny? You mean you saw his future?"

Rachel tilted her head to one side, then slowly shook it. "No. It's more like seeing brief snippets of thoughts and emotions. I searched the scrying mists to help him find the right path."

"And the right path was me?" Harley frowned over the rim of her mug, relaxing into the comforting warmth the spiced wine sent through her veins.

"It's difficult to explain," Rachel said. "What I saw was that your and Ronan's auras were intertwined." She placed her mug back on the tray as calmly as if she'd just discussed the weather.

"Auras intertwined. I know what I've read about auras, but would you mind sharing yer definition so I can be sure we're on the same page?" Harley slipped lower in the chair, her eyelids becoming impossibly heavy. She'd never tolerated alcohol well. The least amount made her as sleepy as a porch cat stretched in a patch of sunshine.

Rachel shook her head and moved to help Harley up from her chair. "We'll talk of that another time. For now, I think we'd best be getting you into bed. You're exhausted."

Harley barely stifled a yawn as she stumbled along beside Rachel. "No, really. I'm fine. Tell me about the auras. Or at least about mine and Ronan's. How could you see my aura when I wasn't even here?"

Rachel led her to the bed, turned back the covers, and gently forced Harley down onto it as if she were a stubborn child. "We are all connected. All of us are a part of the energies of the universe. No matter where or when we reside."

Giving up and pulling her feet under the covers, Harley sank into the welcoming pillows. "So, even though I was far into the future, you still saw Ronan's aura and mine were connected?" She rubbed her eyes with both hands, struggling to stay awake. "Have you ever seen other auras intertwined as you called it? Connected like mine and Ronan's?"

Rachel smiled. "As a matter of fact, I have. Just one other time. When I looked into the scrying mists and saw mine and Caelan's."

CHAPTER 10

Aveline smiled at the images in the flickering blue haze floating above her outstretched palms. She didn't care what the others said. She knew she was doing the right thing.

Brisk footsteps echoed in the hallway just outside the door of Mama's solar, making Aveline drop her hands to disrupt the spell. Her mother was already unhappy with her. She didn't need her questionable spell casting discovered.

As soon as the door burst open and Mama pinned her with a stormy scowl, Aveline knew she was in for an extended lecture the likes of which she had never endured before. She pulled in a deep breath and braced herself. The best course of action to survive the lecture would be to say as little as possible.

Her mother circled her, eyeing her while snorting exasperated little huffs that reminded Aveline of their Highland bull. She fully expected Mama to paw the ground at any moment. "Aveline—" Her mother's tone spoke volumes. "How often have we discussed the need to watch what we say regarding *anything* involving our mystical gifts?"

Taking care to keep her eyes downcast, Aveline chose words that wouldn't further stir her parent's wrath. "I thought since Harley came from the future; she wouldn't be shocked by what I said. I hoped it would ease her into settling in."

Mama huffed another heavy sigh. "Just because Harley is from the year 2008, does not mean she is any more accepting of the supernatural than the people of this century. It's going to be difficult for her to fit into this time. And from what I've gathered, she was somewhat of a loner in her time and didn't rely on anyone but herself. In this era, very few women can pull that off with any success. Many have tried and not lived long enough to tell about it."

"But she doesna have to be alone," Aveline said. "All she has to do is accept Ronan. I know he'll be happy with her. I've seen it." She bit her lip and stifled a groan. She should not have said that.

Her mother stormed closer, shaking a finger in time with each clicking step. "What have you seen? And what have I told you about practicing scrying without the protection of another in the room?"

Aveline backed away, wishing she'd kept her mouth shut as she'd planned. She had no choice now but to confess. One never lied to Mama. "I only took one quick look into the mists. Nothing came at me while I was there. I wanted to help them—to help Ronan—move along into what is meant to be."

"I have told you many times that the visions absolutely cannot be used to manipulate people." Mama's face flushed red with irritation as she paced the length of the room. "You never know if what you see is to be, or what could be, and at what cost the action might cause. You could unknowingly cause your brother harm without understanding what lies just outside of the border of your vision. What if you sent him down a path to utter destruction because you didn't know the entire effect of what you put into play? Every action is like throwing a rock into a pond, the ripples travel far and touch unknown things."

Aveline swallowed hard, trying her best not to cry. What had she done? Panic, dread, and worry filled her, nearly choking off her air. Even though Mama had lectured her many times, she had never thought about her abilities that way. She would never do anything to cause Ronan harm or unhappiness. She only wanted him settled, so maybe he'd stay home more and not be constantly at sea. The keep was so lonely whenever he was gone. She missed his laughter. He left a void in their family that was so hard to bear.

"I am sorry, Mama," she whispered, staring down at the floor. But Goddess Brid help them all, it was too late for her actions to be undone.

Her mother pinched the bridge of her nose and wearily shook her head. "What have you done, Aveline? Tell me everything so we can make sure nothing goes awry."

~

STILL GROGGY WITH MORNING SLEEPINESS, Harley became aware of someone moving around the room, their footsteps softly scuffling across the rugs, then lightly tapping whenever they happened across the exposed wood flooring. She opened her eyes to the narrowest slits and spotted an older woman setting a tray overloaded with covered plates on the table beside the hearth. At least it was someone safe creeping about the room. That made her breathe easier. She scooted herself upright against the headboard and hugged her knees. "Good morning," she said. The rich, buttery scent of warm baked goods filled the room, making her mouth water.

"Ah, ye be awake." The thin matron, her gray hair pulled back in a tidy bun, smiled and bobbed a curtsy. "Good morning to ye, mistress." She returned to preparing a plate. As she spoke, she waved a knife dripping with butter. "My name is Ellen. I be the one to take care of ye whenever ye be needing a thing, and I am honored to have been asked to do so."

Harley eyed the lady, impressed by the efficiency with which she bustled about the room and conquered several tasks at once. But what did Ellen mean by *taking care of her*? She was neither an invalid nor a child. The MacKays needed to realize she was perfectly capable of taking care of herself. She eased out of bed and gave the lady a polite smile. "It's good to meet you, Ellen, and you can call me Harley." She arched a brow at the mountains of food stacked on the tray. "My goodness. Surely, all that isn't for me. You'll eat some too, I hope?"

"Oh, no, mistress." Ellen chuckled and shook her head while patting her trim waist. "This fine breakfast is all for yerself." She eyed Harley with a thorough once over. "They said ye were thin, and they nay lied. Why, ye are a mere shadow." She shook a finger at her. "Winter will be upon us soon. Ye'll be needing some meat on those bones to keep from freezing." Her henlike clucking at what she obviously felt was Harley's neglect of her health filled the room. "Why, yer waist is so small, I'll be needing to take in every dress by at least a full hand. And look at yer poor arms—thin as sticks, they are. For one so tall, ye are no bigger around than my wee granddaughter of barely ten and two."

"I am perfectly healthy and have been this size for years—no matter how much I eat." Her parents had often teased her about eating like a wolf but looking like a greyhound. Harley selected a steaming scone slathered in butter, placed it on a small plate, then settled into a cushioned chair, and curled her long legs under her. "My father used to tell me I was a panther in a past life and carried the lean, lanky look into this one."

Ellen paused and studied her again, tilting her head to one side as she nodded. "With those golden eyes of yers, ye do look a bit like the sleek lions on the tapestry in the main hall." She added another generous dollop of honey to a steaming cup. "Yer tea, mistress." She set the cup and saucer on the table beside Harley's chair. "Once ye finish that scone, I'll dish ye up a fine bowl of parritch made all the richer by adding plenty of cream, butter, and honey. As I said, winter is coming, and I intend to add a bit of meat to those bones of yers. Cook and I willna have ye freezing on account of us."

A purr of contentment almost escaped Harley as the buttery scone melted on her tongue. Maybe she could allow herself to be *taken care of* for just a little while—at least until she got her bearings and learned the lay of the land. She sipped her tea and stifled a gag. "Wow." After smacking her lips, she ran her tongue across her teeth. The cloying sweetness of the tea was thick enough to slice.

"Uhm...could you add a little more tea to this cup of honey? I appreciate your efforts and am thankful you're here, but it's a little too sweet."

Ellen huffed a disgruntled snort as she added a little more tea to the cup. It was quite apparent she considered the duty of increasing Harley's dress size her own personal quest. "Lady Rachel sent a dress for ye, and I gathered the underpinnings needed to go along with it. Yer dress, underthings, and slippers are behind the screen along with a pitcher of fresh water, linens, and soaps." She made a face. "Lady Rachel said ye would most likely wish to tend to yer own washing rather than be proper and allow me to do it." She shrugged. "Whatever ye wish, mistress."

"I would. Thank you." Harley preferred not to even think about Ellen scrubbing her down. After finishing her scone, she walked behind the screen and came up short at the wooden chair with a hole in the seat. Even though she knew what she would find, she peeped into the hole and wrinkled her nose at the sparkling clean chamber pot waiting on the shelf under it. Lovely. An indoor outhouse. She bit her lip, staring at the thing while her bladder insisted she get a move on and use the antique convenience.

It seemed like she peed forever. Which she decided was a good thing, because that would make for fewer visits to the wooden toilet. She tried not to think about what would happen when *other* business became necessary. More of the same, of course, but the fresh bag of large green leaves hung on the arm of the chair would leave a lot to be desired when it came to cleaning up after a number two. She shuddered to think of the ordeal her next menstrual cycle would entail.

"One battle at a time, Harley," she muttered under her breath. The pitcher held cold water. If she wasn't awake before, she was now. She gritted her teeth to keep them from chattering as she washed with what felt like ice water.

The stories were true. Castles in Scotland were indeed drafty. And perched on a cliff above the sea, Castle MacKay was not at all overly warm even though it was early summer. Or she assumed it was. It had been back in Kentucky, and what little she had seen of the land from the lookout tower had appeared green and teeming with life.

She didn't tarry with her ablutions, just warmed herself by briskly toweling dry, then turned and eyed the *underpinnings*. Ellen had stacked them on the small table beside the vibrant crimson dress hanging from a wooden peg hammered into the privacy screen.

"Nothing for the bottom half other than stockings," she said to herself, as she held up what appeared to be an antique bustier, a shapeless dress along the lines of a white cotton nightgown, a pair of stockings, and ribbons that she wasn't quite sure how to use. "I should have taken that course on historical fashion for an elective," she said as she put the stockings and ribbons back on the table to have both hands free to attack the corset. "Does this thing tie in the front or the back?" she called out to Ellen.

"The front, mistress. I thought it best since Lady Rachel informed us that where ye are from, ye tend to be quite shy and private—preferring to do things for yerself—rather than allowing me to help as is proper."

Harley smiled. Obviously, Ellen did not approve of a lady handling her more personal matters herself. She wondered where exactly Rachel had told everyone she was from. Shaking her head at the thought, she slung the corset around her back, pulled the edges close in the front, and struggled to lace the thing as snugly as she'd seen them do in the movies. "This is not comfortable." She turned and eyed her sports bra, then checked the neckline of the dress. The sports bra would never work since the gown appeared to be one of those that somewhat bared the shoulders.

After one last deep breath, she gave up and tied the supportive garment, wondering how long it would take her breasts to spill out over the top. She'd never been the busty sort, but that thing lifted the girls and set them on a shelf for everyone to admire. Stockings next, she decided, then maybe the linen nightgown? Seems like she'd seen a movie once where the women wore that to keep their gowns clean longer by protecting them from sweat and body oils.

She perched on the edge of the wooden toilet, pulled on the

stockings, then stood. With every step she took, they crept downward. The ribbons. That had to be what kept the stockings up. Harley shook her head. "And here I thought they were for my hair."

"What say ye, mistress?" Ellen called from the other side of the screen.

"Nothing." Harley yanked the stockings back up in place, then tied the ribbons around her legs just above her knees. "This feels weird." No underwear, hosiery held up by ribbons lashed around her knees, and a sleeveless straight jacket to keep her chest shelved up under her chin. She donned the linen nightgown next, and while it made her feel less exposed, it did not diminish the strangeness of her *underpinnings*.

"And now, for the dress." Harley pulled it down from the hook, marveling at the richness of the vibrant crimson cloth. She slipped it on over her head and let fall in place. "It fits—perfectly," she called out to Ellen.

"Lady Rachel has a good eye," the matron said, sounding as though she was farther across the room.

It not only laced in the front but also under her left arm. She pulled those snug first, tied them, then tucked the loose ends out of sight. The gown wasn't quite off the shoulder, but it was close. The sports bra would never have worked. Harley frowned at the amount of exposed flesh as her breasts swelled dangerously close to the neckline. Actually, they mounded above the neckline like a pair of softballs ready to pop out and play. She shoved them downward, held tight to the neckline and corset, and hopped up and down, trying to shake everything down to a respectable level.

She emerged from behind the screen, still tucking as much of her chest down into her dress as possible. Head bent and focus fixed on her décolletage, she walked straight into Ronan, then squeaked and jumped back a step. "What are you doing in here? Did you ever think of knocking, or is that something they didn't start doing until the *next* century?" Her cheeks burned like fire, and the heat spread to her chest. She knew without looking she was probably a brighter crimson than the dress.

Ronan stared at her, silent as if carved of stone. Lips barely parted, his gaze raked across her, making her burn even hotter.

"Well? What do you want?" She stamped her stockinged foot and clapped her hands inches from the tip of his nose.

He cleared his throat and pulled himself up to his full, impressive height. "I knocked, lass. Mistress Ellen let me in on her way out. She said ye were dressing and bade me promise to stay on this side of the screen and wait for ye like a proper gentleman."

"A proper gentleman, my Aunt Fannie." While the look in his eyes made her feel beautiful, a feeling she hadn't felt in a very long while, she wasn't about to let down her guard. "What do you want?"

"I thought to give ye a more extensive tour of the keep and the grounds." He cocked a brow and tipped a glance down at her feet. "But ye might not be comfortable traipsing about the place in yer stockings." After a contrite bow, he added, "Ye look verra lovely in yer gown, lass. Verra lovely, indeed."

"Thank you." Her hands went to her hair. "I still have to deal with this, though." She glanced around the room, trying to remember what Ellen had said about shoes or slippers. "As you can see, I am not finished dressing. Why don't you come back later—or better yet, eat something from the breakfast buffet so Ellen will think I ate it." She went back behind the screen and searched. No. No shoes there. Hadn't Ellen said that was where she put them?

His deep, rumbling chuckle filled the room like light from a sunny window. "Aye, ye will find Ellen relentless in taking care of her charges. 'Tis why Mother assigned her to ye. Yer slippers are out here, lass. Beside the bench at the foot of the bed. And yer brushes and combs are on the dressing table."

She rounded the screen to find him on one knee, a pair of leather slippers in one hand and his other held out for her to take. "Allow me to help ye finish dressing, and then I'd be most happy to give ye a complete tour."

Flustered at such gallant attentiveness, she crossed the room and held out her hand. "Give me the shoes. I don't need any help."

With a sly glint in his eyes, he held them just out of her reach.

"Nay, lass. Ye must allow me to make amends for barging in on ye uninvited. I dinna wish ye to think me some ill-mannered cur. Allow me to fit the wee slippers on yer feet, and then I shall brush yer hair." He winked. "Ye will find me gentle and quite talented."

He was goading her. The man acted like making her snap at him thrilled him immensely. Teeth clenched to keep from giving him that satisfaction, she flounced down onto the cushioned bench and held out her foot. Rather than verbally spar, she fixed him with a venomous glare.

With his amused gaze locked with her lethal stare, he cradled her stockinged foot in his massive hand and methodically swirled his thumb in a mesmerizing circle around her ankle. She tensed every muscle to keep from shivering and revealing to him how tantalizing that felt.

As he slid the soft leather of the shoe onto her foot, he gave her the sort of smile that made it clear he could undress her even more easily if she would only allow it. He barely touched the back of her leg, massaging her calf, his fingertips leaving a burning trail through the thin layer of the silky stockings.

With his eyes never leaving hers, he gently lowered that foot to the floor and slid his hand in a soft caress along the top of her other foot.

She wet her lips and struggled not to pant. This was so not fair for him to have such an effect on her. His smug smile helped her battle her way out of the haze of his mesmerizing touch. He treated her to another delicious massage before placing the slipper on her foot and securing the ties. Once he finished, she pulled her foot out of his hand and placed it on the floor, primly beside the other one. "Thank you. Now, why don't you eat something while I brush my hair? As you can see, there is more than enough food."

He leaned forward and placed his hands on either side of her, trapping her on the bench while bringing his face closer to hers. She swallowed hard as he held his mouth within a hair's breadth of hers. "I am not hungry for food, lass. Let me tend to yer hair, and then I shall take ye on the tour I promised. And dinna worry. I intend to keep ye close. For yer own safety, of course. A woman as lovely as yerself must be cherished and protected at all times—and I am the man to do it."

She swallowed hard and forced herself to breathe, battling with the urge to lean into him and give over to whatever he wanted. She couldn't. Not under any circumstances. Not until she figured out how she fit into the strangeness that had become her life. She pushed him back and placed one of her feet on the ground between his knees while slowly digging her thumbs into the soft indentations just above his collarbone. "Sweet words, MacKay. But you will find I am not some helpless wench bowled over by empty promises."

He surprised her by curling his lips to one side in a self-assured smirk, then bowed his head and lifted his hands while leaning back to free her. "Ye will find I never make empty promises, Harley—and I would never err by considering ye helpless."

She rose and jutted her chin in the air, then pushed past him, went to the dressing table, snatched up the brush, and started yanking it through her tangled hair. How dare he treat her like some female that only existed to melt in his arms. She'd made the mistake of being vulnerable once. Never would she go down that road again —especially not in fifteenth-century Scotland. She had more important matters than dabbling with *men* to attend to here.

Silent as a shadow, he was suddenly beside her, taking the brush out of her hand. "Nay, lass. Such beautiful hair should never be treated in such a manner. Allow me." He gently took her by the arm and led her to a cushioned stool. "Close yer eyes, Harley. Relax. Ye should know by now that I mean ye no harm."

She knew he meant her no harm, but in a way—he did. He had such a *pull* to him. It wasn't just his dark good looks, either. There was something in his eyes, something unspoken in his words, *something* about him that made her realize she could forgive him a multitude of sins and would delightfully help him commit even more. She cleared her throat, painfully aware that her increased heart rate and rapid breathing were probably quite visible by the rise and fall of her exposed chest. "I'm not tender headed. Sometimes, it snarls so badly you just have to rip it out."

He leaned in close, the warmth of his breath tickling her ear. "Leave it to me, lass," he said softly. "Close yer eyes."

After a deep breath, she shut her eyes and gave over to the gentleness of his touch. The rhythmic shushing of the brush as he ran it across her tresses hypnotized her. "You are quite good at this. Do it often?" She figured he used this method whenever he was in port seducing women.

"Aye, lass," he said with a humorous lilt to his tone. "Every day."

She opened her eyes and lifted both brows. "*Every* day?"

He chuckled as he pulled her hair back from her face and started plaiting it. "When we visit the stables, I shall introduce ye to Enbarr. Ye will see what a fine mane and tail he has because I ensure they are well brushed daily. His hair is almost as lovely as yers."

Without moving her head, she rolled her eyes. He had just compared her to his horse.

He stepped away, gathered up more items from the dressing table, then returned to stand behind her. "These combs will hold this fine braid in a coil to the back of yer head and make everyone see ye as the regal lady that ye are."

Rendered speechless at such a compliment, she struggled to think of something to say, but only came up with a weak, "Thank you."

He rested his hands on her shoulders, leaned over her again, and brushed the most seductive of kisses to the side of her neck. "Thank ye for allowing me to attend to ye, m'lady." The intoxicating softness of his deep voice caressed her senses.

She drew in a shuddering breath and pressed a hand to her flaming chest that she felt certain mirrored her burning cheeks. Time to escape before she did something she regretted. She skittered away from him and went to the door. "Now that you have me ready—" She inwardly cringed at her choice of words. "Let's go."

Ronan smiled, joined her at the door, and offered his arm. The look in his eyes almost dared her to take it.

Far be it from her to back down from a dare. She ground her teeth together and fought to get a handle on both her irritation and fascination with him. She hooked her arm through his, reminding herself she only had to play this game until she was sure of herself and able to survive. Besides, maybe while he was showing her around, they'd pass a short wall she could shove him over. She didn't want him dead —just bounced around a little and put in his place for all the complicated feelings he had no right setting ablaze inside her.

CHAPTER 11

Ronan escorted Harley everywhere she wished to go in the keep, showed her everything she expressed an interest in, from the kitchens—both outdoor and indoor—to the laundry, the dovecote, the guardhouse, the armory, and everything in between. And the more servants, craftsmen, and various members of the clan she met, the more possessive of her he became. She failed to notice the impression she made upon those she spoke with, but he didn't. He tucked her closer to his side. All had better realize this beautiful woman was not to be approached with any intentions other than innocent and honorable ones.

"You don't have to hold me so close," she told him as they left the guardhouse and crossed the bailey. "I'm not light-headed like I was yesterday."

He didn't relax his hold of her in the least. "I enjoy holding ye close." The loveliness of her blush deepened once again. He prided himself on keeping that color high on her cheeks. The deeper the color, the stronger her emotion, and it was her emotions he wanted to stir the same way in which she stirred his.

With a proud tip of his head, he motioned at the next structure. "And here we have the fine stables of Clan MacKay. Do ye ride?" He remembered his mother once saying she had never been near a horse before traveling back to the past.

Harley inhaled a deep breath, as if the pungent scent of the stables was the sweetest fragrance she had ever encountered. "Hay, horses, and well-oiled leather," she said in a hollow tone. "Reminds me of home." She went to the first stall and a roan mare poked an inquisitive nose over the low slung gate. A sadness came over her as the mare quietly whickered a greeting and nudged her hand. "I rode horses almost before I learned to walk. My parents owned a stable for many years before they decided to retire and take to the open road on their bikes." Her eyes took on the troublesome sheen of tears barely held at bay, and she flinched a shrug. "I wonder if they know I'm gone yet. They'll go crazy with worry when they can't find me." She cleared her throat and turned her back to him. "This is quite a stable. Do all of these horses belong to your family?"

Ronan stifled an irritated growl at himself. He was a damned fool. Bringing her to the stables had been a mistake. It had stirred her worries about the life she could no longer have. He would answer her question, then they would leave. "Most of the horses belong to my father and brothers. Neither Mother nor Aveline ever cared much about riding." He gently took hold of her arm and turned her back to face him. "Come, lass. We will go. Forgive me for rubbing salt in yer wounds. I swear 'twas not my intent."

She gave him a forced smile, then her eyes flared wide and her hand flew to her throat. "It can't be," she said, then pointed a trembling finger at a man who had just emerged from one of the stalls. All the color drained from her. Her lips moved, but no more words came out.

"Harley!" Ronan caught her as she swayed to one side. "What is it?"

"It's him." Her eyes rolled up, and she crumpled without another word.

He cradled her limp form to his chest and turned to meet the gaze of the man standing at the mouth of the stall. "What the devil did she mean, *it's him*?"

With a scrub of his hand across the stubble of his chin, the man slowly set aside the hay fork against the stall. "Ask yer sister. I shall be down at the docks should ye need me."

Ronan stared after him as he left the stable. "MacCallen! What have ye done? Ye were told to stay away from Aveline."

⁓

"AVELINE!" Ronan charged into the main hall, bellowing with the strength of everything in his being. Harley still lay limp in his arms. Only her warmth assured him she wasn't dead. Gently, he placed her on a bench in one of the side alcoves and tucked a small pillow under her head. Whatever mischief Aveline had stirred with MacCallen could not be good. And whatever the two had done, it had affected Harley, and the Mother Goddess herself strictly forbade such dabbling in the lives of innocent mortals.

The mysterious MacCallen had been besotted with Aveline for years. Ever since she blossomed into a beautiful young woman, he had followed her around the MacKay lands like a lost puppy begging for scraps. The man appeared grateful just to be near her, and since MacCallen was a drifter with no claim to any clan, he was lucky he got as close to her as he did. But Aveline was soft-hearted and had begged Father to take him in, to give him a place with Clan MacKay. And her being the youngest of the MacKay children, and the only girl, Laird Caelan MacKay always gave Aveline her way.

"Aveline!" Ronan roared again as his mother came running from the kitchens.

"What are you bellowing about?" She wiped her hands on the cloth tied around her waist. Shock filled her face when she spotted Harley. "What happened? What did you do?" She rushed to Harley's side and knelt, pressing her fingers to her throat and moving her lips as she silently counted the beats of Harley's heart.

"What did *I* do?" Ronan thumped his chest with both fists. "Not a thing, but it would seem MacCallen has, because as soon as her eyes fell on him, she fainted dead away, muttering something about *it's him.* When I tried to get an answer out of MacCallen, he said I best be asking Avie!"

Rachel slowly rose to her feet and wrung her hands even tighter in her apron. "Perhaps you better go up to my solar and speak with Aveline. What she has to say will answer your questions."

His blood boiling with rage, he scrubbed his face with both hands. He dreaded discovering what his little sister had done this time. Aveline had always held a special place in his heart, but if she had meddled in Harley's life, destroyed it, even, he didn't know what he would do.

"How bad is what she did?" He fixed his mother with a leery glare.

Rachel bowed her head and released a heavy sigh. "Extraordinarily bad. She intended to speak to you about it today as soon as you finished visiting with Harley."

Without further comment, he turned, stormed across the gathering room, and took the steps of the stairwell two at a time. Not bothering to knock, he kicked open the door to his mother's solar, knowing his sister expected him.

"Now, sit down and let me explain. 'Tis really not so bad as it seems." Aveline approached him with a carefulness that served her well. She cringed the closer he drew to her. "Dinna be so angry. I promise everything will be fine. 'Tis not good for ye to fly into such a rage, brother. Take deep breaths and find yer calm."

He clenched his fists and widened his stance, bracing himself for whatever foolishness she had set loose upon the world this time. "Let me be the judge of just how bad yer actions are, little sister. Speak. Now."

"Well, ye ken how lonely ye've been?" Aveline gave him a smile that only made him angrier. "The last time ye were home, ye even told me so yourself. Even said the sea didna bring ye the comfort it once did."

Clenching his teeth so hard his jaws ached, he narrowed his eyes at her, silently bidding her to confess the rest.

Aveline shrugged and gave him another weak smile that quickly faded when he ignored it. "Well, ye ken Mama taught me how to work with the Mirrors, and call up the scrying mists." She shuffled in place, a sure sign she knew just how badly she had erred this time. "Well, brother, ye weren't the only one feeling lost and alone. I came upon Harley in the future and discovered she needed comfort and relief as much as yerself." She clasped her hands behind her back and wet her lips, rounding her eyes wider with a feigned innocence that no longer suited her. She twitched a shrug. "I thought the two of ye needed each other and brought her to ye. But I had to use MacCallen's help for the spell."

"Ye were the one who brought her here?" Of all the things his little sister had ever done, this had to be the worst. Her arrogance and disregard for the ancient laws astounded him. "Harley was trapped inside Cliodhna's locket. Do ye mean to tell me ye bargained with the sea goddess herself, as well?"

Aveline shuffled in place again. "Sort of. But I handled everything just right, and MacCallen helped me word the pact carefully. Ye dinna do the goddess justice, ye ken? She is quite reasonable if ye listen to what she has to say."

Ronan bowed his head and sucked in several deep breaths to keep from shaking Aveline until her teeth rattled in her empty little head. "The gods and goddesses are sly, ye wee bratling. They only seem reasonable until they twist yer words, and ye discover yourself caught in a pact ye would never wish to keep."

Aveline balled up her fists and stomped her foot. "I am not some fool who doesna ken a toadstool from a tadpole. The only pact I must keep is to ensure that the sea goddess is never forgotten. All I have to do is tell my children—who will tell their children, in turn, and so on. See? I told ye, I had it all figured out."

He turned his back on her and stared up at the ceiling, wishing the answer to this mess was etched somewhere in the heavy wood beams that spanned the length of the room. "The goddess will allow ye to think ye have made an easy pact, and when ye least expect it, she will show ye where ye were a wee fool. And what of MacCallen?

What did ye promise him? Ye already made him a home here in Clan MacKay."

Aveline shrugged and glared at him, clearly befuddled. "He helped me because he's my friend. He's grateful to us for giving him a home."

"Aveline! How can ye be such a fool?" Ronan slammed his fist on the table so hard that the candlesticks bounced off onto the floor, making the candles hiss away their flames. "MacCallen wants ye, Avie. As a man wants a woman. And ye being the laird's daughter makes ye even more appealing."

Dismay filled her eyes as she backed away from him. She flipped a hand as if to wave away his words. "Mama wasna even as enraged as ye are. Ye should thank me for finding the way to end yer loneliness, for working out a way to bring the two of ye together. I've seen the happiness yer joining will bring."

"At what cost?" Ronan spat. "Ye ken as well as I that it is forbidden to meddle in another's life without their consent. Of all the rules ye ever ignored, ye turned yer back on the cornerstone of every rite ever taught to us." He gave her a hard shake. "Ye are to harm none, Aveline. Harm none!"

"But I didna hurt her!" Tears streamed down her face, but anger had replaced the dismay in her eyes. She was angry because he wasn't grateful to her, and sorry she'd gotten caught—not sorry that she'd violated the ancient edicts. "I harmed none!"

"Harmed none?" he roared. "Ye tore her away from her life. Took her from all she knew and cared about and dropped her into a century where she knows nothing about survival. Ye may not have done her physical harm, but what ye did to her emotionally—'tis unforgivable." He pushed her away, shaking his head at her selfishness.

"Ye will both thank me someday!" Her tears ran faster, and her face reddened even more. Aveline had never been one to see more than one perspective at a time—and her perspective always took priority. "She was miserable in her time. MacCallen confirmed it when he traveled there to trap her in the locket and bring her here.

She had nothing. I brought her back here to be with you, so the two of ye could be together!"

"Why, Aveline?" he asked through clenched teeth. "Ye never do anything for another. How did ye benefit from this madness?"

She scooped a candle up off the floor and threw it at him. "Because I wanted ye to stay home! I'm tired of ye always being gone to sea. Ye were the only one who ever listened to me and didna tell me to go somewhere else and play!" She crumpled into a heap on the floor and covered her face with her hands. "I thought if I found ye a wife, ye would stay here and make babies. Then I wouldna be so alone.

He wearily dropped into a nearby chair and leaned his head into his hands. How could she do such a thing? Snatched an innocent woman out of her life and dropped her right into the middle of theirs. His mother had always said Aveline's powers would be the greatest, and that she would be the most difficult to guide and control. There was only one thing to be done. He hated the thought of it. But it could not be helped. He lifted his head and glared at her. "Ye must send her back. I dinna ken how or what ye worked out to bring her here, but now ye must make things right and send her back."

Aveline hugged her knees and shifted in place with an anxious back and forth rocking. "I canna do that. I already sealed the pact with Clíodhna. Once done, nothing can be undone. 'Twas one of her terms on which she wouldna negotiate—even MacCallen couldna sway her on that point." She wiped her nose on her sleeve and shrugged. "And he swears he'll not tell Harley what we did. We can just tell her she's mistaken about having seen him before. His glamour in the future was of a much older man. I'm sure we can convince her she's never met him."

Ronan jumped up from the chair and glowered at her. "No. Ye will tell Harley the truth. I will not give MacCallen anything he can use against our clan. Ye have done enough damage by being deceitful. Telling more lies will only make it worse."

He yanked her up from the floor and stared deeply into her eyes.

"As soon as she awakens from her swoon, ye will tell her everything, ye ken?"

"She'll hate me." Aveline clutched at his sleeves, nervously plucking at the material. "She doesna ken a thing about magic. She'll never understand."

"Ye will be lucky if that is the only punishment the Fates and Goddess Brid place upon ye." Ronan shoved her away and stormed out the door.

CHAPTER 12

Harley sidled her way down the staircase, her back pressed against the wall, moving with a silence born of sheer desperation. She didn't have a clue as to where she was headed, all she knew was she had to go. For the last unbelievable hour, she had listened to Aveline, and she'd be damned if she stayed around to be manipulated by the MacKays anymore.

Ronan, Rachel, and Laird Caelan had stood on either side of the sniveling young woman, their heads bowed and faces dark with anger and shame.

Awestruck into silence, Harley had sat there, staring at Aveline, unable to believe anyone could be so selfish as to hatch such an outlandish plan. If not for the fact that she sat in Scotland in the 1400s, she would have thought Ronan's sister was insane.

As soon as Aveline had tearfully hiccupped out her story—for that was how it had come across—like some twisted fairy tale, not a confession or apology. Harley had stared at her for a long, heart-stopping moment, then bolted for her room. She'd locked herself inside and pressed her back against the door, ignoring Ronan's incessant hammering and pleas to open it and let him in. She'd shut her eyes and gritted her teeth until he'd given up and left her alone.

A raw, somehow wrong sense of pride in staying strong against him had filled her—still did. He was the one thing in all this chaos that she didn't want to leave. Her pirate Highlander had an inexplicable pull to him. He drew her in like a moth to a flame. Well, her wings had been singed before, and thanks to Aveline, they now smelled a little burnt again.

And now it was time to go. She had to get out. At this point, the where of her plan would be figured out as she went along. If she survived this century, great. If she didn't, well, she'd decided if that was her fate, then so be it. She'd never been a coward before and wasn't about to start now. All she knew for certain was she could not spend another minute under the same roof with the person who had ripped her away from everything she had ever known.

Ellen had laundered and neatly folded her jeans, cotton pullover, and twenty-first century *underpinnings* and placed them on the top shelf of the wardrobe. Her sneakers were there beside them too. Harley had carefully returned the borrowed dress to the peg on the screen and donned her clothes, thankful that the opinionated yet kindly maid hadn't discarded them.

Now, the back staircase to the outer entrance Ronan had shown her earlier in the day served her well. With any luck, that friendly little mare from the stable would allow herself to be saddled for an unscheduled ride into the night. Harley loved animals, always had, and they always loved her. Hopefully, that sweet fifteenth-century beastie wouldn't be any different.

The outer bailey was silent, with only the occasional shadow flitting across the cobblestones as a clansman standing watch upon the battlements strolled beneath the light of the waning moon. She melted into the shadow of the wall until she was positive the guard had crossed to the other side of the tower. With a tight hold on the dark plaid around her shoulders and hugging her supplies to her chest, she stole across the yard to the stable door. She paused and strained to hear if anyone was inside. Satisfied at the quiet within, she slipped through the door and was greeted by the curious whickering of the mare she'd met earlier in the day.

"Hello, friend," she crooned softly to the horse. "I'm happy to see you too. How about we go for a moonlight ride?"

The roan mare perked her ears, as if anxious for an adventure.

Harley ducked under the stall's bar and hurried to saddle the amicable beast. She tied her cloth bag of supplies—bread, dried meat, and a skin of water—to the saddle, then mounted the patient mare. During her flight out of the keep, it had occurred to her that filching the food and stealing away appeared to be going entirely too easy, but she would take it. "I'm due some good luck. Hopefully, karma remembers I'm not such a bad person and helps me out." Once seated in the saddle, she leaned over the animal's neck and stayed low as they slipped across the yard and exited the gate.

That was another thing. The MacKays had a guard walking the wall but left the portcullis up and the wooden gates open? Was that standard Scottish defense? She glanced back over her shoulder, squinting at the window of the guardhouse. The guard was right there, watching her, but didn't sound the alarm. She peered harder. There was a tall, shadowy figure behind him, watching too. But neither said a word. Maybe the MacKays wanted her gone as badly as she wanted to leave. Fine by her. That made her exit easier on all of them. Although, it did kind of hurt her feelings. She'd truly thought Ronan was as drawn to her as she was to him. She shook her head. "Stop it. It's better this way, and you know it."

She urged the horse to a faster pace in case whoever was in the guardhouse changed their mind. Once they galloped across the bridge spanning the narrow ravine, she released the breath she'd held since spotting the watchers in the guardhouse. "Come on, little mare. Let's find a nice, quiet place to lie low for a while."

A moonlit trail prompted her to veer to the right and head for the coast. If memory served and her history lessons were the least bit accurate, most settlements would be along the shore. She glanced down at her apparel and had second thoughts about not bringing along the fifteenth-century clothing to fit in better with any population she happened to find. Her jeans, pullover, and sneakers would be hard to explain. She rolled her shoulders and shook the worry away. "I'm not going back for clothes. I'll figure it out."

An eerie feeling of being watched made her twitch her shoulders again. She pulled the mare to a halt and twisted in the saddle, looking all around while listening for the sound of someone following. Nothing but the steady shushing of the nearby waves hitting the shore came to her. No movement caught her eye. The nearby woods concerned her a bit. Someone could easily hide in those shadows the trees provided.

"Move, if you are there," she said under her breath, while staring at the darkest part of the forest. Nothing happened. The only movement was the trees shifting in the wind.

"I'm paranoid." But after all that had happened, she had the right to be. She urged the horse onward, noticing the trail gently sloped downward, and the hard packed dirt was softening with the addition of a sandy loam. The steady music of the waves got louder, and when she rounded the last huge outcropping of boulders, she discovered she'd escaped to a deserted horseshoe bay that led to nowhere.

Harley eyed the tiny deserted bay and shook her head. "Well, dammit."

She dismounted, tied off the reins to a scraggly bush, and walked farther down the beach to make sure she wasn't mistaken about the bay. With another shake of her head, she returned to the mare. "You could've told me we were headed for a dead end. I thought we were friends?"

"She knew it was the safest place to take ye. Friends take care of one another." A huge black stallion stepped out from the shadows beside the mound of stones and touched noses with the little mare chewing at what leaves she could reach. Astride the great horse, dressed all in black, was a scowling Ronan, glaring at her with his hands resting on the lip of the saddle.

Harley's heart geared up to a hard, pounding rate, making her swallow hard. She squared her shoulders and shifted to put the mare between them. "Go home, Ronan. I am no longer the responsibility of you or your family."

"Like hell ye're not." Dismounting in one smooth, powerful move, his dark cape billowed out behind him. It snapped in the rising wind as he slowly strode toward her. "'Tis not safe for ye to travel alone. I have come to bring ye back."

"I'm not going back. Go away." She kept her gaze locked on him while trying to untangle the reins from the bush. Everything had been going so well—until now.

His eyes were dark and unreadable, his mouth hard and unsmiling. His approach never slowed. He stalked toward her like a hunter determined to capture its prey. "Ye will come with me. Either willingly or not. I will be damned straight to the hottest parts of hell before I allow ye to ride off to some unsavory fate because of yer sheer bullheadedness. I have had my fill of women who think they can do as they damn well please without giving a care as to the consequences. We will begin anew, ye and me. Somehow."

Burning rage shot through her from the top of her head to the tips of her toes. "*Women who think they can do as they damn well please?* Your sister stole my life away, and you dare lump me in with that self-serving little beast? Go home, MacKay! As I said, my fate is no longer your concern and as far as your *fill*—you can shove it."

Lightening split the clouds roiling in to blot out the light of the moon. Deafening thunder crashed like boulders dropped from the sky, shaking the ground. Glancing up, Harley stared in bewilderment at the quickly rising storm.

With one great stride, Ronan closed the distance between them and jerked the reins out of her hands. He grabbed her by the shoulders and lifted her off the ground, forcing her to meet his gaze. "Aye, my sister stole yer life. But I'll not stand idly by and allow ye to throw the rest of it away. Ye will return with me whether ye like it or not."

Harley kicked hard, landing a solid hit to his groin. As he doubled over, she brought her knee up under his chin and knocked him back onto the sand. "As I said MacKay—shove it!"

Just as she recovered the reins to her horse, she found her feet jerked out from under her. Ronan yanked on her ankle, pulling her toward him. She scrabbled flat on her stomach, then rolled in his grasp and kicked at his face.

Growling like an enraged beast, he caught hold of her free foot, crawled his way up her body, pinned her shoulders in the sand, and forced her to meet his glare. She kicked and bucked, trying to dislodge him, growing more enraged the longer he held her down. Hands full of sand, she threw it into his eyes, causing him to shift his weight. As he bellowed at her success, more lightning and thunder shattered the skies. The clouds opened, sending rain and hail pelting down.

She finally bucked free as he was trying to clear the dirt from his eyes. Scuttling away on her hands and knees, a roar of rage ripped free of her throat as he grabbed her ankle again and dragged her back to him.

As the storm built and the rain sluiced down, he grabbed her hair, forced her head back, and stared down into her face. He narrowed his eyes and thunder once again shook the earth as he crushed his mouth onto hers.

His lips were hard and unrelenting as he worked her mouth open wider, claiming her with a determination she'd never experienced before. He crushed her against his chest and stroked the line of her jaw as he drove his tongue deeper, demanding her to yield with every possessive thrust. This was not just a kiss. This was a vow, a bonding that neither time nor tide would ever erase. The connection both staggered and thrilled her. They *clicked*, for lack of a better term. He was the missing piece to her puzzle—the part she had always searched for, the part she needed to be complete.

When he lifted his head and stared down at her, the fiery resolution in his eyes shook her to her core. "Come with me. To my ship," he said, his voice deep and raw with passion. It was neither a question nor an invitation, but a call to war if she chose to rise to the challenge.

An urgent breathlessness spurred by panic and pure unadulterated lust made it so hard to think, impossible to be logical, rather than animalistic. She fought to ignore the raging inferno he had kindled. If she gave in to him, then what? She was not a subservient woman of this century. She would never be the sort to bow her head and accept whatever a man said—no matter his handsomeness or the possessiveness in his eyes.

She was already so vulnerable. So unsure of herself. But the way he looked at her, the way he held her, she hadn't felt this connected to another human being since—ever. She needed him. A shuddering breath escaped her. She needed him a damn sight more than she was ready to admit. Did she have the courage? Would she rise to the challenge?

"Fine," she whispered. "I will go with you—just this once."

He inhaled deeply and locked her in a hypnotic stare. "*Domum recurro,*" he uttered, then touched his forehead to hers.

The air around them crackled as though electrified. A myriad of colors whirled around her. She squinted her eyes shut against the dizzying energy and tucked her face against the warm, muscular curve of his throat. She had to escape the strange, blinding haze.

Then the luxurious softness of a feather mattress cradled her. The plump firmness of a lush pillow was tucked under her head. She opened her eyes and found herself staring into Ronan's watchful gaze.

"Where are we?" she whispered, afraid to look.

"On my ship."

Was he as dangerous as his sister? Would he attempt to manipulate her if she didn't do what he wished? Her heartbeat roared in her ears, threatening to make her retch. "You do magic too?"

"Magic is a part of me. But never a part ye should fear. I would never bring harm to ye, Harley, or use it to force ye to bend to my will." His dark brows drew together, pain and regret shadowing his gaze. "I swear to protect ye for all of my days." He smoothed her wet hair out of her face and softly ran the heel of his thumb across her bottom lip. "I am sorry for all that has happened, lass." He seemed to be battling with himself. "But it would be a lie if I said that I was sorry ye are here." He pressed his forehead to hers again. "I need ye, Harley. I am drawn to ye—and heaven help me if ye ever cast me aside."

She turned her head away. Unshed tears of uncertainty burned her eyes. How could she trust him? Was it just duty making him say these things, or did he really want her? If it was only duty, that would soon fade. She had been down the road of empty promises before.

He gently forced her to face him. Ever so softly, he tasted her mouth—a precious caress this time with the subtle promise of so much more. He pressed tender kisses to her eyelids and nuzzled his way to the tender flesh behind her ear, all the while barely trailing his fingertips along her collarbone. "Trust me, lass. Dinna fear I will hurt ye or ever cast ye away. I promise—as retribution for my sister's selfish ways—I will always protect ye and stay by yer side."

And there it was. Duty. Paying for his sister's sins. His words doused her fires as effectively as an ice bath. She even shuddered. "We are done here. I need to find the little mare and take her back to the castle." She shoved him. "Get off me. Now."

"What?" He stared at her, his face a storm of disbelief. "But, Harley—"

"Let me up. Nothing is going to happen between us. Not now. Not ever. I appreciate your oath and all that—and if you want to protect me the rest of my life? Fine. Do—whatever." She pushed up from the bed and yanked at her wet clothes, doing her best to straighten them and wring them out. "But that's it. I do have some pride, and pity sex is something I'll never need. Not from you. Not from anyone."

"Pity sex?" He scowled at her, glaring at her like a caged animal about to escape and eat its captor.

"Yes. Pity sex. As in, you intend to sleep with me because you feel it's your *duty*." She jutted her chin higher. "When a man makes love to me, it's going to be because he loves me—*not* because he feels guilty over some stunt his sister pulled."

"I assure ye, lass, my need to make love to ye doesna fall under the heading of *duty*. I need to be joined with ye. I ache to make ye mine."

She arched a sleek brow and tilted her head. "So, you're saying that even though you've only known me a scant few days, you find yourself madly in love with me?"

He clenched his fists at his sides and the sound of rumbling thunder grew louder once again. "At the moment, I would say I'm finding myself sorely tried by ye and ready to turn ye across my knee and smack yer arse for ye!"

She tossed her wet hair and headed for the door. "Good. As long as you're just as miserable as I am, there might be some hope for this century yet!"

As she crossed the ship and stomped down the gangplank an enraged roar back in the captain's cabin battled for supremacy over the deafening thunder shaking the land.

CHAPTER 13

Harley paused in her brushing of the mare, closed her eyes, and pressed her forehead to the horse's warm neck. "Thank you for being my friend and listening," she whispered.

The sweet beastie whickered softly, as if reassuring Harley she would always be there for her.

The stables had become a sanctuary of sorts, a safe haven. It was the only place where she could connect to her past in this difficult century. Several days had gone by since her and Ronan's stormy bout. Everyone in the keep from Laird MacKay to the kitchen maids tiptoed around her, avoiding eye contact, and when they *did* speak to her, it was in the soft, pitying tones used for those who weren't quite right in the head. Well, of course, she wasn't quite right in the head. What the devil did they expect? She hoped they continued to leave her alone. Wallowing in self pity was a solitary task that kept her too busy to engage with anyone. As long as she had the mare to confide in—she'd get through this just fine.

But the electrifying scenes of days ago kept nagging at her, taunting her with dangerous memories. The thrill of Ronan's determination to keep her. The warmth of his hard, muscular body on top of her, a deliciously perfect fit. Those strong, callused hands of his that touched with a tenderness that tempted her to forget everything else but him. He possessed the power to take her mind off the past—no doubt existed about that.

"Ye should give this time a chance, Mistress Harley. Ye may discover here and now is when ye shouldha been born."

She glared over the horse's back at MacCallen where he leaned against the roughly hewn post of the stall. His dark blue eyes narrowed as he glared back at her. A snort escaped her, and she resumed the rhythmic brushing that brought more comfort to her than to the contented little mare. "I cannot believe you'd think I'd ever listen to a word you had to say ever again. Not after what you and that conniving little brat did to me. Do us both a favor, why don't you? Stay as far away from me as you can get."

MacCallen scratched his beard while fixing Harley with a scolding look that tempted her to throw the brush at him. "Sweet Aveline heard yer words of loneliness by the river. I heard with my own ears how the man ye intended to wed spurned ye. Are ye truly so miserable here that ye're filled with hatred for this time and everyone in it?"

After placing the brush onto the shelf, Harley edged her way out of the stall. "No. I do not hate everyone here. Only a select few have earned that place in my heart, and congratulations, you are one of them." How dare he play judge and jury over her life. She might not have been the happiest person at that particular time. But it was still her life, and neither he nor Aveline had any right to take it away from her. Of course, she never would have met Ronan, had they not—but that was another complicated matter that she hadn't quite sorted out. What Aveline and MacCallen had done was still wrong.

MacCallen pursed his lips and leaned back against the stall. "If ye feel ye must hate anyone, then I proudly accept yer fury. But I would ask ye to give wee Aveline another chance. The lass meant well."

Harley gritted her teeth as she unrolled the sleeves of her white tunic and tugged the wrinkles from the linen. "I have nothing to say to Aveline, and if she's finally found herself in possession of some sense, she better not say anything to me." Tossing her heavy braid back over her shoulder, she dismissed him by heading for the door. "And I recommend you keep your distance too."

∽

WITH HER ARMS hugged around her knees, Harley sat perched inside one of the squared embrasures of the battlement, idly gazing at the sea. The snug crenel formed by the roughly hewn stones was the perfect size to cradle her with a merlon at her back and her feet wedged against the next one in line.

Scotland was beautiful. There was no denying that. From the rugged coastline of what she now knew to be the northeastern Highlands to the heather covered crags and rolling hills and meadows in between. The land soothed her. Almost made her feel welcome. She blew out a heavy gust of air. Perhaps it was time she came to terms with her new lot in life and made the best of what lay ahead.

She swallowed hard at the sudden knot of emotions making her throat ache. If only she could've seen her parents one last time. A tear escaped, and she batted it away while clearing her throat. "Just stop," she muttered. No more crying. Her parents were alive and well somewhere in the future, and they had always taught her that no matter what, life went on, and one should always be grateful that it did.

"Make the most of it," she said, repeating their words to the wind. Only thing was, she didn't exactly know how to do that. Another of their sayings came to mind. No matter the circumstances, she always had the choice—be miserable or joyful. "Miserable or joyful," she said, feeling a tad guilty about holding on to the first one longer than perhaps she should have. Her parents always wished her joy. Happiness. If she couldn't return to her time, the least she could do was honor her parents by living the way they would wish her to.

"Lass?" For some reason, the familiar deep voice didn't startle her. "I dinna mean to intrude, but I worry for ye." Ronan stepped out of the shadows, his face dark with concern.

She shrugged and forced a half-hearted smile. Time to practice what her parents always preached. "I'm all right. Just mulling things over and realizing I've been a little slow to remember the childhood lessons I learned from two amazing people."

"Ahh..." He nodded as he moved closer and leaned against the wall beside her. "Ye miss yer parents. I am truly sorry, lass." He dropped his chin to his chest, frowning. "Seems I say that to ye every time we come together and yet, it is never enough." He lifted his head. "But I am more sorry than ye will ever know."

A nearby torch along with the moon lit his features—spotlighting his earnestness and sorrow. He truly regretted what had happened to her. It rolled off him in great waves of remorse.

"It's not your fault," she said, and meant it this time. She tore her gaze from his, fearing his power to hypnotize her without even trying. She wet her lips, hungry to feel his mouth crushed against hers yet again. It would be so simple right now to throw herself into his arms.

Without a word, as if sensing she needed his touch, he slowly reached out and brushed a stray lock of hair from her face. His fingertips barely grazed her cheek.

She shivered, holding her breath as he ran his fingers up into her hair. Her pulse quickened, pounding in her ears as he leaned forward and nibbled a tender kiss across her lips. Giving in to the hunger he stoked, she opened her mouth wider, slid her hand to the back of his neck, and laced her fingers in his hair.

Ronan lifted her out of the battlement, pulling her into his arms without breaking the kiss. A word formed in her mind as she melted into him. *Perfection.* They fit together like the right key for a lock, like water in a bucket, like sand filling an hourglass.

"Ye set me ablaze, my honey-eyed lass," he whispered against her throat.

She shivered again as the warm softness of his mouth kissed and nipped his way ever lower. *So divine.* A hot, impossible to ignore aching pooled in her core. Belatedly and with a great deal of surprise, her common sense kicked in, reminding her of what might possibly happen and the consequences therein. Her eyes flew open, and she reluctantly pushed on his chest.

He lifted his head and stared down at her, his face filled with worry.

"Before this goes any further," she said, "how do women keep from getting pregnant in this century?"

While relief seemed to flit across his expression, she didn't miss his low, pained groan. "There are ways to keep ye from getting a bairn, lass. But ye have to trust me to have some control."

Control? Seriously? At a time like that? She took a step back and placed more space between them. "If you're saying what I think you're saying, that is one of the most unreliable methods there is to keep me from getting pregnant."

He resettled his stance and glanced all around as if struggling to remain calm. "Harley, we've yet to even make it to the bed, and ye already fear ye are with child."

She folded her arms across her chest and stood taller. "The last thing you and I need right now is a baby. You have to be careful about these things. I may be a virgin, but I know it only takes once, and then it's too late to think about what you should've done."

"A virgin?" he said, as though shocked. "Truly?"

"Yes. A virgin. May I ask why you seem so surprised?"

"Well—" He waved at her with an up and down motion. "Yer age, of course." He clamped his mouth shut, looking as though he wished he hadn't said that. "What I meant was, ye are from the future, and at yer age...Well, I figured ye had already—"

"Keep talking, MacKay...you're digging that hole a little deeper with every word." She pushed past him, grabbed the iron circlet on the door, and pulled it open with a yank. "Your charm and wit are going to ensure you never have to worry about your control. The only way I'll ever get pregnant with your child is if you suddenly become mute!"

∽

Ronan threw back his head and roared, his ragged cry echoing across the land. How could one woman be so infuriating? Just when he thought he had won her trust and brought her close, she shoved him back to where he was when he started—possibly even farther back than that. He'd never had this much trouble bedding a lass, nor wanted it so badly. He went still, staring out at the frothy white caps of the waves. Nay, he did not wish merely to bed her. Deep in his heart, he knew one time with Harley would never be enough. He needed her. For his. For always. He roared again. Damn, if he didn't need her at his side, for ill or for good, until their souls left this life and found each other in the next and fell in love all over again.

The same door she'd slammed in his face opened again, making him turn.

Dagun peeped around the edge of the barrier.

Ronan bared his teeth and growled, then stomped back to the battlement overlooking the sea.

"Heard the battle cry, cap'n. Thought I best come to yer aid." Dagun edged his way closer to Ronan's side. "Be there mischief afoot. Somethin' the crew and I can handle?"

"That woman is driving me mad! That is the mischief, Dagun." Ronan clenched his fists atop the stones, not taking his gaze from the sea.

"I see." Dagun nodded while scratching his chin. "Woman troubles. By my way of thinking, ye would be better served and safer too, tupping one of the kitchen maids. Yer Mistress Harley doesna seem the sort of lass who would take too kindly to an idle roll in the hay." He nodded again. "She'd be one to expect more from ye. Mark my words."

Ronan slowly turned and glared at his first mate, his frustration and rage blinding him. "Who says an idle roll in the hay is what I want? What if I wish to take a wife?"

Dagun threw up both hands and backed away. "I meant no insult to yerself or the lady, cap'n. I just meant...I thought...Hell! Ye ken as well I that I'm no expert when it comes to the fair sex."

Scrubbing his face, Ronan snorted. "Obviously, I am no expert either, or else I'd not be standing here talking to ye."

Dagun thoughtfully tipped his head to one side. "I'm thinking ye would be better served if ye wooed the lass. How do they do it her time?"

Ronan nodded slowly. "Aye, ye may have something there." He turned and headed to the door, pausing long enough to toss a glance back at Dagun. "I think it high time I looked forward with the Mirrors and found out more about Mistress Harley's past."

CHAPTER 14

"I miss the warmth of the mortal's beating heart." The deep voice echoed through the cave at the edge of the sea, drowning out the sound of the lapping waves.

"We agreed to release the mortal to this time. Ye ken as well as I that we canna keep them imprisoned forever. Brid forbids it, and I've no wish to return to her prison." Goddess Clíodhna's melodic voice trickled through the crevices of the cavern, like water gurgling across river stones. "Besides, what of the one ye have watched and nurtured for so long? Is she not ready to join ye? She is of age now."

A rumbling rose from deep within the stones around the cave as though something powerful struggled to bubble to the surface. "I have as yet been unable to win her heart. It would be so much more pleasing if she wished to join with me of her own accord. I wish it to be her choice to be at my side. Not my own."

"Bah! Mortals never know their own minds. Trick her to make her choose. Ye ken her weaknesses as well as I do. Surely 'twould be no feat for the God of the Sea to woo her in a way she couldna refuse." Goddess Clíodhna's haunting laugh vibrated through the cave, her voice taunting.

The sides of the cavern shook with a slow trembling. The ground beneath the waves shuddered and rolled. "Dinna think I dinna ken what ye are about, Clíodhna. I am nay the fool. All ye wish for is the return of yer adoring wee mortal. Ye are jealous of how he yearns for the one we brought to this time."

A spray of white foam shot through the cave as though fighting for more space. "Brid has forbidden me to reclaim my sweet Ronan. I dare not touch him lest she banish me from this realm permanently. But there is no protection for the one he desires, and the one ye seek is yet to be punished for breaching the sacred law set forth by the Fates."

Deep, rumbling laughter filled the salty air, vibrating through every tunnel and turn. "We will work together, yerself and I, Clíodhna. In so doing, we shall each gain that which we desire."

"Aye, old friend. We shall each have our mortal amusements to bide us through the epochs of time." Then the tide reversed, and the gods washed out of the cave as quickly as they washed in.

~

RONAN SLOWLY LOWERED his arms to his sides, erasing the images from the Mirrors of Time. His heart ached at what he had just witnessed. How could anyone treat his precious Harley in such a callous manner? Blatantly lie to her? Humiliate her and play her for a fool? He rubbed his chin while replaying the scenes of Harley's past through his mind. That cur she almost wed had wounded her deeply. It explained a great deal about her leeriness toward men.

Then MacCallen had trapped her with the guise of an elderly man. Ronan clenched his fists, envisioning his hands wrapped around that fickle bastard's throat. When the locket had sucked her soul into its wee prison, his frustration with his thoughtless sister made him hunger to cast her into the locket's chamber to see how it felt. Aveline was fortunate they had been able to restore Harley and free her, else her transgression against the sacred laws would have been deemed even worse. The Fates and Goddess Brid had yet to pass down their punishment, but Ronan knew without a doubt they had not forgotten about Aveline and what she had done.

He loved his sister dearly, but she had never learned that with great powers comes great responsibility. That basic tenet had been ingrained in all the MacKay children at an early age. But with headstrong Aveline, the lesson had been lost.

Now that he had looked into Harley's past, Ronan knew exactly what to do. She needed to be wooed. Both her trust and her heart would have to be won, and he was determined to do it. He didn't know for certain when he had decided to make Harley his own. Perhaps it was when he opened his eyes to find her lying in his arms upon her release from the locket. Or maybe it was the way she had fought him on the beach. Remembering her fire made him smile. It didn't matter when he came to the conclusion he needed her. All that mattered was that what he felt for Harley was more than just a passing desire. She was his other half. His one true mate—and he didn't need the MacKay curse to know it.

Ronan took the stairs two at a time up to her room. He stared at the door a long moment before knocking on it. Muffled stirrings came from the other side. She must've been lying down. He resettled his footing, wishing she would hurry and open the door.

Ellen jerked open the door. "And just what do ye be wanting, Master Ronan?"

Disgruntled at finding himself facing the elderly maid rather than Harley, he peered past her into the room. "Where is Mistress Harley? Did she not retire after the evening meal?"

Ellen scowled at him, then planted her fists on her bony hips. "The mistress has gone for a stroll of the grounds. She thought it might calm her mind and help her sleep."

"A stroll of the grounds?" He narrowed his eyes at the wily matron's smug expression. "She is out there alone?"

"Did I say she was alone?" Ellen clucked like an old hen, then toddled back across the room and started tugging and smoothing the bed coverings.

"Then who is she with?" He charged after her, taking every step she did as she flitted about the room, preparing it for the evening. "Ellen—I bid ye answer."

She snorted. "Ye bid me answer? I used to help yer mam clean yer bum when ye shite yerself. Dinna be thinking about pushing yer bidding with me, Master Ronan. I answer to my laird. Ye ken that well enough."

"Who is she with?" He struggled not to raise his voice, knowing it would make the old cow dig in and be even more unhelpful.

"'Tis none of my business. Your father has spoken to us more than once about engaging in idle gossip. He'll not have it, he said. Wise man, our laird. He knows how tales can fester and boil until they scorch some poor, innocent soul." She ignored Ronan while filling a pitcher with hot, lavender-scented water.

"Ellen—it is not idle gossip if ye are the one who saw who went with her on her stroll." Reasoning with the old woman had always been a chore, and it had become none easier with age.

Ellen shook her head as she plumped the pillows and stacked them against the headboard. "Nay, Master Ronan. If ye wish to know who's keeping Mistress Harley company, ye will have to find that one out for yerself."

With an exasperated snarl that did nothing to make him feel better, Ronan stormed out of the room, down the back stairs, and shot outside. He scanned the outer bailey to see if Harley was there. She had taken to checking in on her little mare before she went up to bed each evening. But the only movement in the yard was a bit of straw blown about by the rising wind. Harley and her companion must be in the gardens. The thought of her meandering through the torchlit plots of vegetables, herbs, and flowers with a man other than him set his blood to boiling. If Latharn or Faolan thought to pursue her, he would have their heads on a pike.

"She is mine," he growled soft and low through his clenched teeth.

As he rounded a wall leafy and lush with vines of ivy, he heard the low murmuring of voices. Keeping to the shadows, he leaned in close and strained to pick up every word of what the evening strollers had to say. He peered through the leafiness of the vines, relieved that it was not another man with Harley, but his mother.

"So, there is no such thing as condoms yet?" Harley sat beside Rachel on a stone bench, plucking leaves from a stem and dropping them into a bowl in her lap.

"I'm sure there are in China—but not Scotland yet. Scots have no idea what a condom is for." Rachel leaned forward and snipped off a bushy top from a nearby herb that Ronan couldn't make out. "The next best thing I found was a bit of sea sponge soaked in oil of tansy. Make sure it's inserted deeply before..." Rachel smiled and tipped her head. "You know. If not for that little trick, there is no telling how many little MacKays would've been running around here, creating chaos along with Aveline and the boys."

"A sea sponge soaked in tansy oil? Seriously?" Harley frowned down into her bowl, picked up another stem, and stripped the leaves from it.

Insert where? Ronan wondered. There could be only one place, and he couldn't imagine Harley putting it there. And what the devil was a condom? What did all those things have in common? He shifted positions and strained to hear more. This must be some sort of new spell his mother had worked out on her own. Some sort of spell to do with womanly things—but what? Their monthly courses?

"I've also heard talk about using beeswax," Rachel said. "But I'm just not too sure I'd trust that in the heat of the moment. If you know what I mean?" She playfully nudged Harley with her elbow.

"Well, that sort of is another problem. I *don't* know what you mean." Harley blew out a heavy sigh, almost cringing as she looked at Rachel.

Ronan frowned. Why would she cringe like that? She and Mother appeared to be getting along well enough.

"Surely, you're not still a virgin?" Rachel asked.

Harley sat straighter and glared at her. "Why is everyone so surprised when I say that?"

Feeling a bit sheepish, Ronan cringed. He had not handled that news well with Harley at all.

Rachel frowned and turned toward Harley. "Who exactly do you mean by everyone? That's not the sort of subject that you bring up with just anyone in the 1400s."

Harley rose and paced back and forth in front of the bench. "Your son—Ronan. He seemed shocked as well. Said something about *my age*. What exactly have you told them about the future?"

"Might I ask how the subject of your virginity came up with my son? Or is that the reason for all the questions about birth control?"

Birth control. Ronan nodded, full understanding dawning as he remembered how worried Harley had been about getting with a bairn.

With her arms set across her chest, Harley tilted her chin to a defiant angle. "I was saving myself for the man I was to marry—for the one who truly loved me. The thing was, the jerk was so understanding about no sex until marriage because he was banging my best friend!"

Rachel rose and hugged an arm around Harley's shoulders. "It's a horrible thing when the one you think you love hurts you. Your fiancé sounds a lot like my first husband."

Harley narrowed her eyes, her gaze centering on Ronan amid the ivy leaves. "Someone is watching us."

"Shite," he whispered. How had she spotted him?

Rachel looked right at him and crooked a finger for him to come out. "It is rude to eavesdrop. Did we not discuss this breach of manners when you were a child?"

With disgruntled surrender, Ronan emerged from the shadows. "I was merely checking on Harley to make certain she was safe—during her evening stroll."

Rachel bent and retrieved the bowl of herbs. "Then I shall leave you to accompany her the rest of the way. I'm sure your father is wondering where I am." She winked at Harley and mouthed *sea sponges* before she turned to go.

"Sea sponges?" Ronan repeated while watching his mother head back toward the keep. After she disappeared inside, he turned back to

Harley and grinned, waiting for her to explain why she was talking to his mother about not getting a bairn.

"Never mind," Harley said. "How did you know I was out here? I thought you were in Emrys's study."

With his most disarming smile, he offered her his arm and waited for her to take it so he might escort her up the lane. "I finished my studies, then found myself a bit lonely. 'Twas my hope ye wouldna mind having some company for a while."

She fixed him with a look that plainly called him a liar. "I am honored." Her tone dripped with sarcasm. "I'm sure a man like you has a woman in every port. Especially the port he calls home." She narrowed her eyes at him. "You spend all your time here at the castle. Is she one of the kitchen maids?"

Clenching his teeth, Ronan fought to hide any reaction to her boldness. The little minx was baiting him. She chose her words with the same care a warrior used to choose his weapons. "Actually, up until recent days, I had no interest in any of the women here. 'Tis rare for me to stay ashore this long, and rarer still for me to stay in my home port any longer than a few days."

She gripped his arm tighter, obviously irritated that he hadn't taken her bait. It made him ache to unleash a victorious smile, but he didn't dare. Instead, he led her through the farthest gate and took the path nestled against the side of the castle overlooking the sea. With a tip of his head at the dancing waves, he drew in a deep breath and gusted it back out. "It calls to me, ye ken? The salty wind in my lungs. Open sea. 'Tis freedom unlike any other."

Harley relaxed against him and smiled. "It's so beautiful here. How could you ever leave all this? And your family too? The MacKays seem a close-knit group who care about each other."

"We are close," he said as he took her hands and gently turned her to face him. "But my life was out there—in search of someone I needed even more. Someone made to understand me as I was made to understand her. Someone to share in my love of the sea. Until I found her, I had no respite from my wandering ways. I had to keep searching."

She hitched in a breath and wet her lips with a nervous swipe of her tongue. "And have you found this someone?"

"Aye," he said softly, locking his eyes with hers. "She is all I ever wanted—ever needed—and even more than I dreamed possible. There is but one problem standing in the way of my happiness." He drew her closer and cupped her face in his palm.

She wet her lips again and appeared to swallow hard. "And what is that, exactly? What is standing in your way—between you and this person you've searched for all this time?"

He brushed his lips across hers and lowered his voice to a husky whisper. "The lass canna see that my heart is pure. She willna allow me to show her how wonderful we two could be."

A soft moan escaped her, and she thrilled him by pressing closer. "How wonderful the two of you could be?"

"Aye, love." He nuzzled tender kisses along her jawline and gently sucked on her earlobe until she moaned again. "Wonderful to share a life together. Share one heart, one soul, one love." Then he claimed her mouth with his and deepened the kiss to make it clear he intended to possess her. He crushed her close, shuddering as her body molded to his. When she melted against him, when the pounding of her heart tapped into his flesh, he lifted his head and stared down at her. "Trust me, Harley. That is all I ask. Let me show ye how easy it would be for ye to love me."

"I want to trust you," she whispered, her voice trembling. She reached up and combed back the wild strands of his hair tugged free by the wind. "You are so different from any man I have ever met before. Can I really trust you? Will my heart be safe with you?"

Tightening his embrace, he lowered his head and brushed his lips across hers as he whispered, "I swear to ye, upon my verra heart and soul, I will never hurt ye."

She laced her fingers into his hair and pulled him in for a hard kiss. The way she poured herself into him made him groan with the need to take her—the need to melt into her and never rise again.

Struggling for the control he knew he had to command, he lifted his head and eyed the moon's position in the sky. "The hour is late. I'd best get ye back to yer room. Back to yer bed."

Her eyes half closed, she leaned into him. "I am definitely ready for bed." The passion in her throaty tone nearly undid him.

Ronan gifted her with a wistful smile, then tenderly kissed her forehead. "I will be leaving ye to yer room by yerself, lass."

"By myself?"

"Aye, love. By yourself."

She scowled at him like a petulant child. "Why won't you stay?"

With a firm tuck of her hand into the crook of his arm, he drew in a deep breath and snorted it out. "I willna lay with ye until I have had more time to gain yer trust. 'Tis only proper that I do so."

"Here I am—finally ready to divest myself of my virginity, and you decide to turn all noble on me?" She glared at him and jerked on his arm. "Is something wrong with me, or is this just payback for the times I've left you high and dry?" She pulled free and blocked the path so he couldn't pass until he answered.

Ronan threw back his head and laughed. "Trust me, lass, the only thing wrong with ye is that I'll not be able to sleep until I've had a long swim in the icy waters of the sea." Unable to resist teasing her, he caught her up in his arms, lifted her off the ground, and slowly spun her around. "And maybe 'tis a wee bit of *payback,* as ye put it, for the times ye've—what did ye say? Left me high and dry?"

With mischief and a tad bit of wickedness in her eyes, she nibbled a slow series of kisses across his mouth, making him hold his breath to keep from groaning. "While you're swimming, would you do something for me?"

"Anything, lass. Name it."

"Find me some sea sponges. A lot." Then she wriggled down out of his arms and bolted away, her laughter trailing behind her.

Ronan kept his gaze locked on her fine backside, regretting his decision to be *gallant.* He would get the lass her sea sponges. Enough so they could lock themselves away and lose themselves in each other's arms till well after Hogmanay.

CHAPTER 15

Perched on an outcropping of stones, Aveline stared at the endless stretch of sparkling blue water that almost seemed to mock her. She hated the sea. Always had. If not for its hold on Ronan, she never would've ended up in this mess. If not for the seductive call of those waters, he would've stayed at the castle like a good brother should. Then she would've never searched through the ripples of time to find a woman capable of keeping him at home.

With the ever-increasing glumness foisted upon her by the wait for her punishment, she glanced up at the gathering clouds and pulled her plaid tighter around her. It had been almost two months since Harley had *arrived*, and Ronan still hadn't forgiven her for so unceremoniously yanking Harley back to the past. Her parents were still angry as well and concerned about what repercussions the MacKay clan could expect from her unorthodox actions. With every act involving the tapestry of time, the rules were set in stone. Unfortunately, she had tossed caution to the wind when she'd manipulated Harley's life.

Aveline stared down at the shore, surprised that the waves had risen so much higher. It wasn't time for high tide. Each wave crashed to new heights, slowly and methodically pulling toward her. Spray shot up and doused her before taking the form of a voluptuous woman who shimmered like the pearlescent inside of a rare and perfect shell.

"Goddess Clíodhna!" Aveline bowed her head and kept her gaze lowered.

"I have watched ye, child," the goddess said, "and seen the plan ye set in motion has not brought ye the results ye wished." The immortal stood at the edge of the sand, the sea foam swirling about her feet.

Aveline wrung her hands together and risked a glance at the goddess. "No one understands I was just trying to help. They're all accusing me of being a selfish meddler."

Clíodhna's laughter bubbled like the waves at her feet. "I understand, child. Immortals frequently face the same accusation."

With her plaid clutched close, Aveline carefully climbed down from her perch and hesitantly approached the goddess. "What can I do to get them to forgive me? Ronan is still so angry, he rarely speaks to me."

Gliding along the water's edge, Clíodhna bent and picked up a tangled rope of seaweed. She idly trailed it through her glistening fingers as she gave Aveline a calculating smile. "Perhaps ye should return the lass to her time? Maybe that would set things right."

"But ye refused to allow that in our pact." Aveline shrugged. "And even if, in yer benevolence, ye changed yer mind and allowed it, I am barred from entering Emrys's library, forbidden to use the Mirrors of Time, and Mama says no more magic until we see what punishment I'm meted from the Fates."

"But if ye put things back as they were before, would that not be making everything right? Perhaps, even make yer punishment less?"

Goddess Clíodhna's lilting certainty gave Aveline the hope she so badly needed. She quickly nodded in agreement. "That would have to make things right. But I dinna ken how I can manage it without the Mirrors of Time. Emrys would surely catch me if I tried to use them."

The goddess gave her a reassuring smile. "The autumnal equinox will be upon us soon. Ye know the veils of time are easily folded then.

Since ye are such an innocent and loyal child, I shall be happy to help ye power yer spell."

A brightness and joy she hadn't felt since Harley's arrival filled Aveline. "Ye would do that for me? I would be ever so grateful. Maybe then Ronan could find it in his heart to forgive me."

Clíodhna nodded her silvery head as she extended her shimmering hand. "Aye, child. I shall help ye reverse this transgression. And in return, should I call upon ye in my time of need, ye will assist me. Do we have an accord?"

Aveline quickly took the Goddess Clíodhna's hand and bobbed her head. "Oh, aye! I will assist ye in whatever ye shall need. I shall ever be yer faithful servant."

"Good," Clíodhna said, as she turned back toward the sea. "Until the equinox then, my trusting child. Rest easy. All will be well."

Aveline clapped her hands as the sea goddess gracefully sank into the waters. Her heart was so light, she danced in circles across the beach, only pausing when a deep, satisfied laugh rumbled up from beneath the waves. Movement made her turn and stare into the shadows beneath the shelf of the washed-out embankment. Were those eyes? An eeriness stole across, making her tighten her hold on the plaid and run up the hillside toward home.

∽

"Something is not right." Rachel stared out the window, unease and a worrisome unrest nagging at her with the relentlessness of time and tides.

Caelan glanced up from grinding the whetstone along the edge of his claymore. "What do ye sense, my love?"

She shook her head while worriedly picking at the cord of the tapestry she'd pulled back from the window's edge. "I don't know. But there is an imbalance in the energies. A quickening of sorts, and it's not anything good."

"The Fates?" He rose from the bench and propped his claymore against the hearth. "Do ye think they have chosen Aveline's punishment?"

She struggled to find the words to describe the malevolent breeze. "No." With a slow shake of her head, she narrowed her eyes and concentrated on the eeriness in the air. "It is not the Fates. This is— different. Threatening. And slowly gaining strength."

A chill that had nothing to do with the weather settled across the room. As she eased down into her chair beside the hearth, she stared into the fire. "Aveline seemed happier today. Almost as if she was relieved."

Caelan's broad shoulders sagged, and he ran a worried hand through his graying hair. "Surely, ye dinna think the lass is up to something yet again? Has she learned nothing?"

"The only punishment she has received so far is her brother's anger. His ire never affected her very much when she was a child. What makes you think it would affect her now?" Rachel flinched as though in pain. "What if she thinks the Fates have let her off?"

"But we banned her from doing magic. Kept her from Emrys's room and the Mirrors. Forbidden her to use any of his tools. What the hell else could she do?"

Rachel rose and leaned against the hearth, idly poking at the burning logs with an iron rod. "Aveline may have finally realized what I've told you all along." She gave a defeated shake of her head. "She is the strongest among us in the ways. Her ability to access the energies is phenomenal. Aveline doesn't need any conductors to concentrate her powers. All she needs is her will and her mind."

"God's teeth," he muttered. "Must we lock her away?"

"You do not understand," Rachel said. "We cannot stop or control her—no matter what we do."

"Then ye'd best be calling out to the Goddess Brid." Caelan threw open the chest at the foot of the bed and drew out her finest candles for connecting to the mighty goddess. "Since Brid is the one who foretold of her powers, perhaps she can bring her under control."

CHAPTER 16

Her heart was as light as the wind in her hair as they galloped across the fields. Harley couldn't resist tossing a teasing glance back. Ronan's black stallion could easily overtake her little mare but for his restraining hand on the reins. He was obviously letting her win, and judging by his joyous expression, did not consider it a loss.

They reined in their horses beneath a sprawling oak, both laughing with the exhilaration of the run. She smiled to herself as she compared riding the horses with the freedom her parents had found on the open highway with their motorcycles. Now she understood their excited connectedness, especially when talking about their times on the open road.

She untied the plaid from her saddle, unfurled it, and let it float down across the ground. Ronan fetched the skin of wine, bread, cheeses, and apples Ellen had packed for them in a cloth knotted at the corners.

"She packed so much." Harley arranged the food on the cloth, knowing they would never eat all of it. "I wish she'd understand I do not need fattening up."

Ronan laughed and settled down beside her. "Ye might as well give up, lass. When Ellen gets something in her head, there is little room for anything else."

"I believe you're right." She snuggled into the curve of his arm as they reclined back into the huge gnarled cradle of roots that made the perfect armchair.

The horses meandered close by, finding their contentment beside a tasty overgrowth sprouting up beside a gurgling burn of the clearest water. A peaceful meadow stretched out past the stream, golden seed heads of the waving grasses mesmerizing as they rippled in the breeze.

A sigh of contentment slipped free of her. She'd finally made peace with her fate. Maybe this wasn't exactly the life she'd expected to live, but the longer she was here, the more she realized that perhaps this was where she should have been all along. She leaned her head on Ronan's shoulder and sighed again.

"Ye seem happy," he said as he brushed a strand of hair out of her face. The tickle of his fingertips, even from such an innocent act, immediately ignited a fiery response within her.

"I am happy." *And aching for you*, she silently added. He had made it painfully clear that until he fully won her trust, *or served his time*, she thought to herself, there would be no dismantling of her virginity.

"Since ye seem happy and contented—perhaps it is time I gave ye this and asked ye to be my wife." He opened his hand and revealed a delicate bracelet made from woven strands of gold, silver, and copper. The intricate knots of the weave interlocked with no beginning and no end, forming a beautifully symbolic band. He slipped the cuff onto her wrist, his fathomless eyes locked on hers.

She stared at the work of beauty, then looked up at him and gave herself fully to the emerald storm of emotions in his gaze. He loved her. More than life itself. It wasn't what he said that mattered. He told her more when he said nothing at all. His actions and the way he looked at her—they told her everything she needed to know.

She meant to speak. Really, she did. But the words wouldn't come as she stroked the band encircling her wrist. As she admired it, first angling her hand one way and then another, all she could do was press her other hand to her heart and blink hard and fast to hold back the happy tears. The precious metals of the bracelet caught the rays of the sun and sparked them back with delightful fire. The unending knots made the perfect statement, glowing with a passion all their own.

"It is so lovely," she whispered, finally finding the power to speak.

"Then ye will be my wife?" He touched her cheek, then grazed the heel of his thumb across the curve of her bottom lip.

"Yes," she said. "Most definitely." She reached up and touched his face, giving herself over to everything she felt for him, knowing and finally understanding that with his mystical senses, he would feel everything she felt. "I know without a doubt that I love you with all my heart."

His eyes flared open wider, then blazed with the same insatiable yearning she knew must be burning in hers. He pulled her into his arms. "My precious love." His hoarse whisper fanned her need for him as he hungrily nuzzled the curve of her neck while sliding his hands across her, stroking and caressing as he trailed kisses along her collarbone.

She guided his head lower and arched her back, closing her eyes as he tickled a path to her nipple with his tongue. "I ache for you," she said aloud. Or maybe she didn't. At this point, she didn't care. All she did was *feel*.

He teased and deliciously tortured her with the tip of his tongue, cupping her breasts and worshipping each of them in turn. With her fingers knotted in his hair, she pulled him harder against her. A shuddering cry worked its way free of her as he sucked her hardened nipple deep into his mouth.

As he slid his hands lower and rucked up her skirts, she clung to him, wrapping a leg around him, and thanking fifteenth-century Scotland for its lack of panties that would only get in the way. He lowered her back onto the plaid while sliding a hand up her inner thigh. It tickled, but, then again, it didn't. She pressed into his touch, needing relief, needing him to take her where she so badly needed to go.

After one last hard suckling of her nipple, so hard that it made her shriek, he lifted his mouth from her breast and crushed it to hers as he sank a finger deep inside her. He swallowed her groans and used the heel of his thumb to tease her throbbing nub while sinking another finger in to join the first. She was about to explode. Or die. Or both. She ground herself into his touch while he worked her into a mind-numbing frenzy teetering on the edge of bliss.

Without warning, he spread his fingers and tore through her maidenhead. She flinched at the unexpected sting interrupting the delicious burn of pleasure.

"Forgive me, love," he told her with a tender, apologetic kiss. "It will be easier now when I take ye."

The fire was still there. The need. An insatiable ache begging to be quenched. She raked her nails down his back and arched into him. "Take me now. I've waited a lifetime for this."

"Aye, love." Baring his teeth, he forced himself inside her slowly, stopping partway.

"Are you in pain?" She stared up at him. "Can we not go faster?"

"I am in more pain than ye could ever know, my precious one." He wet his lips and shoved in farther, then paused and stared down at her.

The muscles of his shoulders knotted beneath her hands and he trembled, making her realize he was struggling to go slowly for her.

"Take me, Ronan—I'm ready. I promise." She bucked upward and tried to pull him down.

"I can hold no longer," he groaned and shoved fully into her.

"Damn!" She tensed, trying to relax around the fullness stretching her where no man had been before.

He drew a ragged breath and looked down at her. "Are ye all right, love? Do ye wish me to stop and leave yer body?"

"Leave my body?" She rocked her hips and arched her back, stretching upward to rub her breasts against his chest. "Are you insane? This is..." She ran her hand down his back and ground her hips upward again. "Carry on—please."

With a growl that excited her and drove her even closer to the climax dangling just out of reach, Ronan pumped into her, faster and harder until he pounded her straight into the heart of ecstasy and followed her to his own release. They matched perfectly, fit perfectly. Their bodies came together as one and completed the puzzle. His roars and her cries frightened the birds out of the trees.

Still shuddering and breathing hard, he pressed his forehead to hers. "I love ye, my golden-eyed lass from the future. Ye have made me complete." He rolled and tucked her close to his side, gusting out a heavy sigh as he did so.

Pressed tight against him, she snuggled her face into the crook of his neck and breathed him in. Satisfied male mixed with satisfied female. Did anything smell any better? She smoothed her hand across his chest, unable to remember when she had ever felt so lusciously exhausted. But then a disturbing thought fought its way through her blissful haze.

"Oh no."

He lifted his head and peered down at her. "What is it, love? Did I hurt ye? Are ye unwell?"

"I forgot the sea sponge." She closed her eyes and groaned. How could she forget the sea sponge?

His brows drew together as he ran his hand possessively up and down her back. "Forgive me, love, but I forgot what ye wanted the sea sponge for."

She frowned up at him. "One little sea sponge, oiled with tansy and strategically placed, helps prevent pregnancy."

His eyes widened, and then he gave her a sheepish grin. "And it appears I failed to keep my promise and find the control to leave yer lovely body when the time came to spill my seed."

"Well." She tipped a shrug. "I'm not so sure I would've let you leave even if you had tried."

He suddenly went solemn and caressed her cheek with such tenderness that it threatened to make her weep. "I love ye, Harley, and the possibility of yer giving me a bairn only adds more joy to my soul."

Her heart swelled so big; it would surely burst if she wasn't careful. She hid her face in the curve of his neck and whispered, "I love you, Ronan. So very much."

He tightened his embrace and pressed kisses into her hair. "I love ye more, my golden-eyed lass. More than ye will ever know."

∼

THE LATE EVENING mist rolled in off the sea, blanketing the cliffs of Clan MacKay. Aveline sat in the garden, her face lifted to the night, eyes closed as she breathed in the chilly night air and concentrated on connecting with the rhythm of the earth. It wouldn't be much longer. Just a few more weeks until the equinox, and then she would return Harley to her time. Maybe then Ronan would finally forgive her and speak kindly to her again rather than constantly scold her.

"I thought I would find ye out here."

She jumped as Ronan stepped out from a shroud of mist and loomed over her. Breath held and bracing herself, she waited, watching him closely. His speaking to her in a calm tone was a promising omen, but not if he changed at the last moment and resumed lecturing her about what she had done to keep him close. She angled her chin higher, knowing she would do everything the same were she to do it all over again. He needed to stay here in the safety of the clan and his homeland. She tilted her head and narrowed her eyes, concentrating on him and the sound of his emotions. He was different. Something had changed. His anger toward her had weakened considerably.

"Ye have changed," she said, the weight of her worry lightening. "I am glad ye are no longer so vexed with me." She scooted across the bench and patted the spot beside her. As long as he didn't berate her, he was more than welcome to sit and offer her the pleasure of his company.

With his hands clasped behind his back, he ignored her invitation to sit. "What ye did was wrong. Ye misused yer gifts, and no, I am no longer as heated with ye as I was before—but that doesna lessen the severity of yer transgressions."

She glared at him. With that attitude and the ability to throw her past mistakes in her face at every opportunity, he would make a good Christian priest. "So, ye merely came to scold me again? Trust me, brother. Mama and Papa have that particular chore well in hand."

Pacing back and forth through the mist swirling around his feet, he frowned downward as though sorting through his thoughts. His demeanor shouted at her, but she couldn't decipher what it was. He was not as angry as before, but he remained anxious about something. But what? And he contained a contentedness and a peace she had never sensed in him before. She sat taller and tensed, beginning to dread whatever it was he was about to say.

"We have yet to hear what yer punishment will be," he said while still keeping his gaze lowered. "Has Mother received any news from Brid or the Fates?"

She blew out a long-suffering sigh and stared down at her hands in her lap. Her read of him was wrong. He was here to lecture her again. She didn't know which she preferred, his sullen, angry silence or his pompous nagging. "No. Mother hasna had any visions as to my punishment. Nor heard from the Goddess Brid."

He halted his pacing, lifted his gaze, and glared at her. "Ye realize that what ye did was wrong? Ye understand where ye erred?"

"Ye canna let it go, can ye? And yes, oh mightiest of my brothers," she said, not attempting to veil her sarcasm. "I have seen my errors and will not make them again, I assure ye."

Rather than lash out at her as she expected, he turned and looked up at the keep and smiled.

Aveline twisted on the bench and followed his line of sight. There Harley was, in the window, brushing out her long, dark hair by the soft candlelight of the evening tapers. Aveline cast a covert glance at Ronan's expression. By the goddess, how he had changed. She had never seen his aura glow with such happiness. "Surely, ye didna search me out to have me apologize to ye yet again."

He turned and gave her a thoughtful smile that tied her middle into knots. She saw it in his eyes. The man was besotted with Harley, and here she was about to send her back to the future. "Avie—Harley and I are to marry. She has agreed to be my wife."

Aveline's heart fell and the knots in her stomach twisted even tighter. Now, what should she do? She swallowed hard and silently thanked the shadows for hiding her worries from Ronan. Thankfully, he also seemed too preoccupied with thoughts of his lady love to notice anything other than his own feelings. If he'd taken but a half second to veer his attention to Aveline, he would have heard her panic fair shouting at him. She had to calm herself, lest he pick up on her worries. She rose from the bench and went to him. "How wonderful! I am so glad the two of ye finally came together and saw ye were meant to be one."

He frowned and cast a dubious look her way. "Ye dinna seem genuinely happy for me, sister. Is this not the reason ye meddled with time?"

Aveline shored up her aura, shielding it from his intuitive senses. "Of course, I am happy for ye. I am merely afraid Harley will not accept me as a sister. After what I did to her life, I fear she will never trust me again."

"I shall speak to her," he said. "She is happy here now, and I am sure she will give ye a second chance. The two of ye will be well on yer way to becoming friends by the time of the autumnal equinox."

"The autumnal equinox?" Aveline nearly choked. Did he know the equinox was when she planned to cast Harley back to the future?

"Aye." Ronan nodded and fell in step beside her as they made their way back to the rear entrance of the keep. "We plan to wed on the autumnal equinox. The veil of time is thinner at that time. We shall be able to project the happiness of our union to Harley's parents."

"But they willna know what it is," Aveline said, quickening her pace as her mind reeled with her brother's news. She had to figure out what to do next. She had to contact Goddess Clíodhna and tell her of Ronan's plans.

He easily kept up with her, his long legs making a mockery of her scurrying stride. "Aye, that is true. They willna know why they feel a sense of peace. But they will know it has something to do with their daughter, and it will assure them she is truly at ease with her fate."

Clenching her skirts in her hands, Aveline quickly stepped across the cobblestones, changing course to head for the steps leading to the outer wall.

"I am happy for ye, Ronan," she shouted back over her shoulder as she scurried down the steps. "Tell Mama and Papa I have gone to the outer wall to make peace with the Fates for the error of my ways."

"I will tell them, Avie," he called after her with a warm chuckle that threatened to make her weep.

She skipped down the steps faster, damning this change of events. She wanted Ronan happy, safe, and at home—if she sent Harley back to the future, he would be none of the three. "I have to tell the goddess. She loves Ronan. Surely, she will allow me to change our plan." But a sickening dread weighed heavy on her and became more burdensome by the moment. Deep in her heart and soul, she knew the goddess would not take this news well.

CHAPTER 17

Aveline hadn't gone to the outer wall even though that was what she had told Ronan. Instead, she waited in the shadows just past the gate until she was positive all but the night guards had gone to their beds. Worrisome guilt nagged at her. She hated lying to anyone but most especially to her favorite brother. He was just now trusting her again, and she feared losing that precious trust once more.

After one last glance back into the silent gardens and at the keep's darkened windows, she hurried to the large, round cobblestone that served as a secret lever to open the wall to the hidden escape passage. It took both her hands and swinging the full weight of her slight body back and forth to make the lever move enough to activate the mechanism. The hidden door finally shifted with a long, low grinding.

She grabbed the sputtering torch from its iron hook and eased down the treacherous steps, made slick with black moss and dark, green lichens. At the base of the stairs, she set her shoulder against the next lever and shoved as hard as she could. A raspy clicking rewarded her efforts. She held her breath as the entrance to the last passage appeared.

With the torch held low to light the damp stairway, she did her best to avoid touching the walls as she descended. The wet chill of the passageway sent a shiver through her. The deeper she descended into the very bowels of Castle MacKay, the more cloying the moldy air became. "Almost there," she said to herself as she pulled her plaid tighter around her shoulders. "And all will be well. The goddess will understand." But the nauseating worry knotted like a stone in the pit of her stomach tightened even more.

At the end of the staircase, she searched for the second torch she knew to be there. With a touch from the torch about to go out, the new torch sprang to life and filled the cavernous room with eerie shadows. It opened into the mouth of an underground bay. The water shimmered like a pool of blackness. Her wise MacKay ancestors hadn't been foolhardy enough to believe their castle impenetrable. So, they had connected their fortress to a cavern that led to the sea. To ensure a safe escape if the MacKays were ever attacked, trusted clan members kept several small boats at the ready at the water's edge. This was the quickest and most secretive way Aveline could think of to contact the sea goddess.

She retrieved the conch shell she kept hidden in the cave and filled it with seawater. With it held high overhead, she closed her eyes and silently called out to the sea, imploring the goddess to grant her another visit. Nothing happened. She opened one eye and checked to be certain. "Please, Clíodhna, please come to me," she whispered.

She opened both eyes this time, fueling her call with every ounce of her power. Finally, the waves within the cavern rippled with an eerie strength and deposited a swirling puddle of sea foam at her feet. The goddess slowly rose from the froth, twisting into her human form.

"What is it, child?" Clíodhna asked. "I not only heard yer cry but also felt yer worry. Have ye forgotten how we plan to make everything right? We've not much longer to wait now. The equinox is nearly upon us."

Aveline found herself mesmerized by the goddess's soothing voice, quiet and shushing like water trickling across stones. She shook herself free of the foggy haze, blinking hard to concentrate.

"Everything has changed. Ronan and Harley are to marry. Nothing must be done." She clasped her hands, squeezing them tightly together as if in prayer. "Please, mighty goddess. Please forgive me for troubling ye, but all is well. Mistress Harley has found happiness in this time. She needs to stay here."

Goddess Clíodhna arched her silvery brows high above her stormy eyes that grew darker by the moment. She gracefully floated along the water's edge, but the foam at her feet churned into angry, frothing bubbles. "And why would ye think that Mistress Harley's happiness is any concern of mine?"

"What?" Aveline went still and an icy dread tightened its fingers around her heart.

The Goddess Clíodhna's essence surged large and powerful, filling the cave and making the waves crash against the stones. "Are ye daft?" She drew her frighteningly beautiful face closer and bared her pointed teeth. "I asked why would ye think that mortal's happiness is any concern of mine? Nothing has changed, Aveline. All will proceed as planned. The woman goes back to the future, and Ronan returns to me."

Aveline bowed and clenched her hands tighter, lifting them in supplication. "Please forgive me. But Ronan and Harley have found love. To separate them now would be truly wrong."

The goddess's menacing laugh echoed through the cave and became deafening as she trailed an icy, wet finger along Aveline's cheek. "Since when are ye concerned with what is right and what is wrong? It didna stop ye from meddling with the fabric of time in the first place to change another's fate—now did it?"

"I...I...should not have done that," Aveline stammered, forcing herself not to stand tall as Goddess Clíodhna's cold, angry face hovered mere inches from her own.

"Then we must make it right. Do ye not agree?" The goddess arched a brow and bared her teeth again in a sinister smile. "We must return everything to the way it was before." Her eyes narrowed into malicious slits. "The woman goes back, and Ronan returns to me. At the equinox, ye will cast the spell as planned."

"Please dinna make me do this, goddess. Please—I canna hurt my brother this way." Aveline dropped to her knees and rocked in place. "Ronan loves her so much. He will hate me forever if I tear her from his side."

Turning her back, Clíodhna slowly disappeared into the ebbing waves. "It shall be done, as we agreed. Call to me no more with yer troubles. The woman goes back to her time."

Aveline covered her face with both hands, choking on her uncontrollable sobs. May the devil take her straight to hell. Ronan would truly hate her now, and her family would never forgive her.

~

"Ye were quite cruel to my little one. I was tempted to strike ye down when her sobs filled the air." The deep voice vibrated through the cave as though the sea scolded the stones.

"Now, now, ye ken it is all part of the plan. We must subtly guide her to seek ye out. She must come to ye to stop me from my evil ways." Goddess Clíodhna's laughter bubbled up through the cave's formations sprouting from its base.

A deep sigh ruffled the darkness, rippling the water into whitecaps and shoving the froth to the shore. "This mortal is special. Her powers are exceptional. I want her to choose me willingly.

"Aye, and ye ken as well I that Brid willna allow ye to take her unless she goes of her own free will. The mighty one protects the MacKays, and even though the child overstepped her bounds, Brid willna allow the family to suffer overmuch for those deeds." Goddess Clíodhna's current form of bubbling sea foam floated on the crests of the waves.

"Brid knows what I feel for this mortal. She is nay against my joining with one so strong in the ways." A deep tidal pool appeared in the cavern, spinning the foam off the water's surface. "What do ye gain from this, Clíodhna? The mortal ye cherish no longer considers ye his only love."

Sea spray filled the air along with Clíodhna's knowing huff. "A mortal's love only lasts as long as the beating of his heart. Once his soul escapes his fragile body, his memory of me is lost. But if Ronan and his wife remember me to their children, sing tales of me down through the generations their love will create, then I will be adored forever as his goddess of the sea."

The tidal pool spun faster, as the rich voice echoed through the darkness. "Then let us hope these mortals play out this game as we plan, so that both of us can find the love and adoration we seek."

CHAPTER 18

Harley tried to ignore the strange smell in the room as she eased another spoonful of soup into Emrys's mouth. No stranger to the sometimes unmistakable scent of the elderly that could be a bracing mix of mentholated rubs, assorted breath mints, mothballs, and sometimes even horse liniment, she had to admit that Emrys's aroma had a tang all its own. Not only did it almost burn her eyes, but also made her nose hairs tingle. It was a strange, sinus-opening smell of vinegar, a hundred and twenty proof alcohol, and aromatic herb clippings that had to have come from the garlic family. She wiggled her nose to keep from sneezing.

"Ye can leave, if ye wish. I can take care of m'self."

"Absolutely not. You've not finished your lunch." She gave him a stern look along with another spoonful of broth.

The old soul had taken a chill a few days back and couldn't quite seem to shake it. From her experiences in the nursing home, she feared the worst for the white-haired druid whom she always thought of as a wizard. Rachel had told her Emrys had been ancient when he'd taken Caelan forward in time over twenty-eight years ago. As to how old he was now, Harley couldn't fathom a guess. She figured he must be at least in his seventies—and for this century—that was quite a feat.

"I am seven hundred and seventy-seven," he said, his eyes narrowing beneath his bushy white brows.

Harley paused with the spoon in mid-air. "That's impossible. And stop reading my mind. You know how rude that is."

Slumping deeper into his pillows, he wrinkled his nose at her. "Ye should know by now that nothing is impossible." He weakly thumped his chest. "I be the master druid and am an excellent cheater of time."

Harley set the bowl on the table beside the bed, sensing he had probably eaten all he could tolerate. She tossed her heavy braid behind one shoulder and eyed him, trying to gauge if he was telling the truth. "Why would anyone want to live that long? Didn't it break your heart to watch everyone you loved pass on?"

His unkempt mustache twitched upward into a shaggy smile. "Thank goodness Aveline chose a woman with some sense to bring love into her brother's life. Most think they want to live forever simply because they fear what's on the other side."

Harley leaned forward and took hold of Emrys's hand. Why do I feel you already know what's on the other side? Can you tell me what you've seen?"

With a wink, he brought a shaking finger to his lips. "Some knowledge can never be understood unless it is experienced firsthand. Why do ye think religion spawns such terrible wars? 'Tis because everything is so grossly misinterpreted."

She gently squeezed his hand. "What I understand is that you need to get better. Ronan and I want you to perform our wedding rites."

"If the goddess wills it, then it will be so. We must bide our time and see." His voice weakened and his eyelids fluttered as he struggled to stay awake. Tell Rachel to stop drugging my broth with herbs. I shall sleep when I damn...well...please." And then he cut loose with a rattling snore and a wheezing sigh from deep within his chest.

Unable to keep from smiling, Harley tucked his hand under the covers and pulled the blankets up to his chin. She truly hoped the old man would somehow conquer this ailment in time to bless the wedding ceremony. There was a priest from a nearby village who would gladly perform the wedding for the son of his laird, but it meant so much to Ronan to have the rites performed by the cantankerous old man he had known all his life—the one he loved like a grandfather.

She glanced around the room, grimacing at the contents of some of the jars on the shelves. A few of those bottles and crocks reminded her of the science lab she had avoided back at college. She wrinkled her nose and squinted at the scrawl of Latin on some of the labels.

As she pushed up from the stool and stretched, she glanced back at Emrys while wandering around the room. He might be weak, but she had no doubt he'd find the strength to scold her for snooping around his workroom and library. She meandered back to the farthest alcove and found herself in front of three of the largest mirrors she had ever seen. At least, she thought they were mirrors. The surfaces were as black as obsidian and polished smooth with a glossy shine. But it took her a few passes in front of them to realize that no reflection appeared inside the ancient frames. "Hmm...I'm not a vampire." She tried to peep behind them, but there wasn't enough space between them and the stone wall.

Each frame was different, intricately carved with eternal knots and symbols she didn't recognize. She admired the design on the frame of the mirror farthest to the right, barely tracing her fingertips along the unusual pattern. As soon as she touched the ornately decorated frame, the black surface of the mirror sprang to life. She backed up a step as faces appeared, then forgot to be frightened and leaned in closer, trying to make out who the people in the image might be. She caught a hand to her throat when she finally recognized Aveline as one of the figures at the center of the scene.

"What is this?" She squinted at the vision as Aveline placed herself between what appeared to be a furious woman and a couple standing so far back that Harley couldn't make out who they were. Ronan's sister appeared to be trying to shield the pair from some sort of harm. Horror made her gulp and back up again as the angry woman changed into a dark, shrouded figure, pointing an accusing hand first at the couple and then at the weeping Aveline.

"Get away from the Mirrors!" Emrys coughed and sputtered as he floundered to push himself up in the bed.

Jumping back as though she'd been burnt, Harley whirled around and faced him. "Dammit, Emrys! Do not scare me like that."

Wheezing for air as he made his way to a sitting position, he sagged back into the pillows and shook his head. "Ye have no training. The Mirrors of Time are not...not harmless toys."

Harley shook her head and waved the accusation away. "I was just looking at them. I thought they were just old mirrors."

Emrys rolled his eyes while still struggling to catch his breath. "Nothing in this room is quite as it seems. Ye would do well to bear that in mind."

Harley pulled her stool closer to the bed while pointing at the mirror that had shown the eerie reflection. "Those images were moving. Was that the future I saw?"

With his chin jutted to a stubborn angle, he stared upward like a spoiled child, refusing to answer. "I barely survived training the MacKay sons and their headstrong sister. I will be damned if I take on the task of training the wives."

"Emrys!" Harley thumped the feather ticking of his bed. "Tell me what's going on. It looked like Aveline could be in trouble. If there's a way for us to figure out when this happens, and what it is, then maybe we can stop it, or change something to alter the outcome to something good rather than bad." She glared at the hard-headed old man, willing him to listen.

"I said no, and I meant it. What ye saw was a mere snippet of time, and those snippets are easily misread." He shook an arthritic finger in her face, his tired blue eyes snapping with renewed vigor. "Tampering with events when ye dinna fully understand them, always makes things worse. Ye of all people should know that."

She jumped up and paced back and forth beside the bed. "Well, I could at least tell Ronan. He's trained and powerful. Maybe he would know what we should do."

Emrys cocked an eyebrow while pinning her with a sardonic glare. "So ye would endanger yer betrothed by enmeshing him in a vision ye dinna understand? Leave the Mirrors alone, girl. Do as I tell ye."

She caught her bottom lip between her teeth. What if Emrys was right? She couldn't bear the thought of endangering Ronan. And the harder she tried to focus the vision in her mind and decipher it, the more confused she became about what exactly she had seen. "Fine. I'll leave it alone. But I can't help but feel it was a warning. Something is about to go very wrong."

Emrys dropped his chin to his chest while slowly shaking his head. When he looked up at her, he gusted a heavy sigh. "It more than likely was a warning since the Mirrors never respond to an untrained touch unless it is most dire. Once I am stronger, I swear to search them myself." He scowled and shook a finger at her again. "What ye should do, lass, is pray I have enough time before that vision comes to pass."

~

HARLEY STOOD AT THE BOW, looking toward the horizon, smiling as the wind tugged at her long dark hair, making it flutter behind her like a dark angel's wings. Ronan unabashedly stared at her, drinking her in, unable to get his fill of her wondrous presence in his world. Gulls cried out overhead while circling the masts, soaring ever higher as the rigging snapped its eagerness to head out to sea once more.

He came up behind her and hugged her back against his chest. With his chin propped on the silkiness of her head, he couldn't remember when he had ever been so content, so complete—and yet, he wanted her again with the same fury he'd burned with earlier when they'd properly christened his grand feather bed in his quarters. Whenever he was with her he raged with the need to join with her and also felt more complete than he ever had before. She was the missing part of his heart. The other half of his soul. There was nothing in this world he couldn't conquer with her at his side. He knew Aveline had ignored the rules of time, but he could not honestly say he was sorry for it. His sister had given him the greatest gift of all. She had presented him with the one he would love, as he had never loved another.

"Will we live here on the ship?" Harley asked, her voice dreamy. "Or will we live at the castle?" She leaned back against him, wriggling in his arms and making him strongly consider picking her up and carrying her back to their bed.

He rubbed his cheek against her hair. "Wherever ye wish to live, my love. As long as I have ye by my side, I care not where we are."

Her fine round arse pressed against him in a most irresistible way as she arched back and kissed him. "Then I choose the sea. The rocking of the ship on the waves adds a very nice rhythm to—things."

A groan rumbled free of him as he deepened the kiss and decided they'd left the bed too soon. When he lifted his head and gazed into her eyes, he gave himself over to their whiskey-colored depths. "Thank the goddess Dagun is my first mate. I dinna think we two shall spend much time on deck."

She pressed a finger to his lips as he started to kiss her again. Her demeanor changed. "Before we—well—before, there is something I need to tell you."

Her hesitancy and the worry in her tone made him stop unbuttoning her tunic. "What is it, my love?"

Her sleek, dark brows drew together in a worrisome frown as she ran her fingers up and down a fold of his léine. "I don't want to keep secrets from you."

"Lore a'mighty, lass. Tell me." What the devil was troubling her?

She patted his chest and peered up at him with the same look he had seen his mother give his father many times. "There is nothing wrong with us. We are perfect. It's about Aveline. And her safety."

"Aveline's safety? What say ye? Last I heard, her punishment still had not been handed down by the Fates."

"Not her punishment." Harley cringed, tensing him even more.

"Harley—tell me. Straight out, my love. Yer emotions are fair shouting at me that something is troubling ye, and it is scaring the living shite out of me. Now, what is it? There is nothing we canna face together." He tucked a finger under her chin and lifted her gaze to his.

"I saw something in Emrys's Mirror," she said softly, as though afraid to say the words aloud. "I think it was something from the future."

Ronan swallowed hard. He'd not expected that. "What did ye see, my love?"

She twitched a shrug and slowly shook her head. "Not quite sure. Aveline was there. And another couple I couldn't see. But the worst part was the furious woman. I mean—I thought she was a woman, but then she sort of changed."

"Changed?" A deep foreboding stirred in Ronan's gut. "Changed how?"

"She sort of—I don't know—morphed into a dark, shrouded figure. Like the grim reaper looking for some souls to gather."

He frowned. Harley's description just confused him more, and this was something about which he needed to be certain. "I would like to try something with ye, love. It might frighten ye a wee bit, but it would show me exactly what ye saw."

She eyed him with a wary frown. "Try something like what?"

He took her hands in his. "I promise ye will be in no danger. But I would like to join with yer mind. See what ye saw."

"Join with my mind?" Her dark brows rose to her hairline, and she backed up a step.

He did his best to calm her by pulling her closer, gentling her with his touch. "Aye, love. If ye will open yer mind to me, then I can see the vision—exactly as ye saw it. I promise to go no further into yer thoughts than what ye saw in the Mirrors of Time."

She studied him for a long moment, chewing on her bottom lip as she narrowed her eyes. He waited. Gave her all the time she needed. This was not something he relished doing, but it would help him understand what was troubling her. She tipped a hesitant nod. "Okay. I'll do it."

Placing his hands on either side of her face, he rested his thumbs against her temples and stared into her eyes. "*Associo.*"

Her hands resting on his chest fisted into his tunic, but in her mind, he took her hand and waited for her to guide him to the vision she had seen in the Mirrors of Time. She smiled at him and pointed at the memory. He studied the figures, their actions, and all their responses. The longer he watched, the tighter he clenched his teeth —until his jaws throbbed. Then he vanquished the image with a wave and closed Harley's eyes with a brush of his hand.

"Was that so bad, my love? Having me in for a wee visit?" He bent and brushed the lightest of kisses across her parted lips. Thankful that during the mindwalk, he'd transported them back into their bed.

She stared up at him from the scattered nest of pillows scented with the sweet fragrance of their earlier loving. "So, what did it mean? Is Aveline going to be all right?"

Ronan pulled in a deep breath and gusted it out in a heavy sigh. "I am not sure. 'Tis my hope that Mother and Emrys can help. What ye saw may be Aveline receiving her punishment from the Fates."

"But who was the couple? The two people we couldn't quite see? It seemed like Aveline was trying to shield them." Rolling over onto her stomach, Harley propped herself up on her elbows and rested her chin in her hands. She aimed her worried frown at the great bay window at the back of the ship, scowling at the rise and fall of the horizon as the ship gently rocked on the waves while docked.

Ronan rose and paced the length and width of the room with his hands clasped behind his back. "I believe the woman—or the grim reaper as ye called her—is actually the Goddess Clíodhna. What I dinna understand is what part she plays in Aveline's punishment, and what exactly she is attempting in that vision."

His eyes narrowed as he stared out the window at the waves. He couldn't ignore the growing sense of unease as he kept replaying the scene in his head. Clíodhna had been furious, but not quite as furious as she was capable of becoming. He had seen her destroy mighty cargo ships with the slightest tip of her head. In the vision, however, it was almost as though she merely pretended to be angry. Her calculated motions were almost theatrical. No. There was definitely more to this than there seemed and acting upon such things was always risky.

"I shall consult Mother. Share the vision with her. If she is unable to untangle the mystery, then we must remain vigilant for when the time of the vision arrives."

Harley rose from the bed and joined him, linking her arms with his as she snuggled against him. "I hope your family's magic is strong enough to protect Aveline from whatever Clíodhna is trying to do."

Kissing the top of Harley's head, Ronan pulled her closer. "So do I, my love. So do I."

CHAPTER 19

The day dawned crisp and clear; the breeze having just enough bite to remind everyone that winter was but a few weeks away. Wispy white clouds raced across the azure blue sky. Gulls circled and cried above Ronan's ship, occasionally swooping down to pluck at the clusters of ivy, heather, and ribbons decorating the deck. Harley and Ronan's wedding ceremony was to be in the bow of Ronan's ship. It was only fitting for their union to be witnessed by the sea.

Amazingly enough, crotchety old Emrys had once again won out over a mere physical ailment and risen from his sickbed in time to perform the ceremony. He wore his finest druid's robes, dark and flowing with every step he took. For once, his wild mane of grey was somewhat tamed and braided away from his face. His beard had also been untangled and smoothed, laying in a shining mass upon his chest. As he idly stared out at the water, he seemed years younger even though he leaned against his staff.

Caelan was garbed befitting a powerful laird. His best plaid crossed his broad chest, while his ceremonial knives were strapped to his trim waist and calves. Rachel's heart fluttered as she eyed her husband's fine form. Even with something as innocent as a wink or a meaningful look, he still possessed the power to ignite her passions.

"Have ye told them?" he breathed into her hair as he brushed a kiss across her temple.

She pressed her lips into a thin, determined line and shook her head. "No. I thought it best to let the pieces fall where they may, since we know how the scene will play out."

"Are ye ready?" He drew her closer to his side, his arm protectively around her.

Her eyes stung with unshed tears, but she forced a smile. "I have to be." She smoothed her hair, fretting with the thick braids coiled around her head. "Brid has shown me this was always meant to be. There is no denying destiny—Fate always has its way."

Caelan hugged her close and pressed his forehead to hers. Today was to be filled with both joy and sorrow. Rachel closed her eyes, begging the powers for the strength to survive it.

"It is almost time," he murmured as he turned her toward the shore where their people had gathered to witness the middle MacKay son's wedding. All eyes were locked on the ship, the smiles of the clansmen almost blinding with joy.

"Ignorance is bliss," she whispered.

"Aye, my love." He hugged her close again. "Take heart. We will get through this."

~

HARLEY FLITTED around the captain's quarters like a nervous moth, unable to stand in one spot longer than a minute or more. She stared out the window, glanced up at the sky, then returned to Ellen who was fuming beside the pile of clothing on the bed.

"You don't think it's going to rain, do you?" she asked the maid. "Do you think it'll be too chilly for everyone as the sun sets?"

Ellen impatiently tapped her foot while fluffing the wrinkles from several yards of lace. "I think that no matter what the weather, ye will never be wed this day because ye willna stand in one spot long enough for me to finish dressing ye!"

With a glance down at the untied state of her stays, Harley caught her bottom lip between her teeth once again. "Oh. Sorry. It's just that I'm a little—I just want everything—I need today to be..."

"Shush now. I know what ye want, and what ye need. Now, stand still, and let me finish lacing yer stays, and then we shall braid the flowers into yer lovely, long hair." Ellen effectively silenced her by yanking so hard on the ties of her bodice that she squeezed all the air out of her lungs.

"I can't breathe!" Harley grabbed hold of the bookcase while gasping for air.

"It is nay that tight," Ellen scolded. "Dinna be such a fractious wee hen." She pulled the gown over Harley's head, tugged it down, then stepped back with a smile. With a happy sigh, she clasped her hands under her chin as the heavy golden silk settled in place around Harley's curves. The color of the gown mirrored Harley's whiskey-colored eyes and perfectly set off the golden glow of her skin.

"You don't think it's bad luck that my gown's not white?" Harley nervously plucked at the fitted waist of the gown. She wanted Ronan to find her beautiful—not looking like a gilded bird in a cage.

Ellen rounded her with the brush in her hand, clucking her tongue as she shook her head. "Ye look an absolute vision, and I have never known Master Ronan to be so besotted. A MacKay doesna count on luck to make his life right. A MacKay believes in fulfilling his destiny. Ye are Master Ronan's destiny, as sure as the sun dwells in the sky."

She soon had Harley's hair plaited into a shining braid coiled around her head and adorned with delicate white flowers. She carefully placed the veil over Harley's face and secured it with intricately carved hair pins fashioned from richly yellowed ivory. "Now ye must wait here until our laird comes for ye." She stole a glance out the window, then shook a finger at Harley. "It willna be much longer. Hold fast, mistress." Then she hurried out the door and closed it softly behind her, leaving Harley to manage the butterflies in her stomach alone.

She rubbed her sweaty palms together and tried to take a deep breath, but was quickly stopped by the tightly laced stays. "I'm going to pass out from lack of oxygen." She reached inside the dress, grabbed the corset, and vainly attempted to gain a little breathing room by giving the thing a hard yank. But Ellen's knotwork was better than any ship's bosun. So, she resigned herself to filling her lungs with one tiny breath at a time.

As the door creaked open, she jumped. Her heart sprang to her throat as she realized it was time. She had only gotten this close to marrying one time before, and that one time had spiraled into a disaster.

"Ye are loveliness itself, lass," Caelan said. "My son has chosen well." He gifted her with a fatherly smile and gallantly extended his arm. "Ready?"

She drew in a shaky breath and laid a trembling hand on his forearm. "As ready as I will ever be."

Caelan chuckled and escorted her out of the room onto the deck.

At the bow of the ship, in front of an arch entwined with ivy, Ronan awaited her with an impatient expression that made her smile. She stopped in her tracks as she eyed the handsome man before her. His dark looks were even more enticing in his finest captain's clothes. His black breeches were tucked into his leather boots that were polished to an ebony luster. His snowy white tunic was open at his tanned throat and his black cloak was pinned with his clan's crest at his shoulders.

Harley felt like she had fled reality and landed in the center of a historical romance novel. The butterflies in her stomach changed into crackling flames of desire. She wanted this man. Both body and soul, and she wouldn't rest until they were united for all to see.

∽

Ronan couldn't help but smile as Harley walked toward him. Her emotions shouted that she wanted him as much as he wanted her. Aye, they belonged together—through this life and all the lives that followed. As long as they found each other and stood at each other's sides, nothing could overcome them. He breathed her in and used his senses to draw her feelings across him. An aching hovered between them, drawing them closer and binding them as one. But it was the sort of ache that promised great joy once it was satisfied.

His mother, Aveline, Latharn, and Faolan all stood to the side of the arch to witness the union. Their signatures on the marriage contract would make it stronger. Ronan huffed a laugh. No contract would make this union stronger. The bond between himself and Harley had been ordained before the beginning of time. He felt it as surely as the air rushing in and out of his lungs. Old Emrys, hale and hearty once more, stood beneath the arch of ivy, waiting to join them after they spoke their vows.

Father gave him a nod of approval before joining their hands and then taking his place beside Mother. Ronan frowned, noticing Father pulled Mother closer, as though shielding her from harm. Surely, he only did that because Mother tended to get emotional at weddings—and was apt to be even worse at her son's union.

Emrys took a golden braided rope from the depths of his robe and loosely wrapped it around Ronan and Harley's wrists. He kept glancing at the sky as if troubled. Ronan gave the old druid a pointed look, silently insisting he tell what he knew. Emrys barely shook his head, then lowered his gaze, and stepped back. No sooner had he done so, when the skies blackened with angry clouds.

Ronan pulled Harley close as the dark thunderheads swirled above the ship, hovering directly above them. Then the realization hit him. The vision Harley had seen in the Mirror of Time was about to unfold. As soon as that thought formed in his mind, a great wave washed across the deck. As the water receded, in its place stood a shimmering woman. It was Clíodhna, and she was not happy.

"'Tis time, Aveline. Cast yer wee spell. It is time ye fulfill yer pact." The sea goddess fixed Aveline with a menacing glare and pointed her pale, shining hand at Harley. "Do it now, child. Lest I lose my patience with ye completely."

Her eyes wide with fear, Aveline stepped in front of Ronan and Harley and defiantly shook her head. "I canna do this. I willna take away my brother's true love. Ye canna expect me to complete this pact."

The Goddess Clíodhna not only swelled in size but darkened with malevolence. "Ye dare defy me? For that impertinence, I shall take both their lives!"

Ronan shoved Harley behind him as Clíodhna roared and pointed a black, shining claw at them. Her evil bellowing stirred the clouds and unleashed lightning all around.

The sea goddess reached for the sky and coaxed the crackling energy into her hands. Her eyes narrowed as she drew that energy into a ball and raised it above her head.

Keeping Harley behind him, Ronan braced himself as Clíodhna hurled the powerful orb directly at them. But a blinding aura of blue-white light surrounded them, protecting them from the lethal lightning ball.

"Enough Clíodhna!" a firm voice ordered from the sky, drowning out the thunder growling through the clouds.

"The accord was broken!" Clíodhna shouted as she pointed at Aveline.

"Aveline will be punished," Brid replied, her shining form materializing upon the deck. Her flaming tresses floated around her, and her emerald eyes snapped in anger. The same blue-white aura that had shielded Harley and Ronan from a painful death glowed around her body.

Calling down more thunderbolts, Clíodhna leered at Aveline. No sooner had she gathered the jagged bits of energy than the Goddess Brid swept them away with a simple nod.

"Ye said she would be punished! It is my right," Clíodhna roared.

Her head tilted to one side, Brid arched a brow at the angry sea goddess. "I think ye best remember that I know of *all* that ye did when ye made the pact with this child."

Her shimmering nostrils flaring, Clíodhna threw up her hands and washed the deck with another crashing wave, then disappeared into the sea. Brid shielded the MacKays from being doused with a flick of her hand.

"Mannanán Mac Lir," Brid called to the shore, her deep green eyes searching the beach and the dock. "Come forward out of yer human form. Come forward to claim yer bride."

MacCallen stepped forward from the throng huddling on the dock. His face was calm as he boarded the ship. Walking slowly to Aveline's side, he took her hands in his. His form seemed to shimmer as he said, "Ye were born immortal. But it was forbidden to tell ye until this place and time. I have loved ye since before the moment ye were created. I watched yer soul before it came down from the stars. Yer punishment is to be bound to me for all eternity for I am the God of the Seas of Time. My hope is that ye will someday come to love me—as I have always loved ye."

Aveline snatched her hands out of his, ran to Caelan and Rachel, and wrapped her arms around her mother's waist. "No! Mama—tell them no! I dinna wish to leave here. To leave my clan and all that I love? Please—just tell them to take away my magic. Please, dinna make me go."

"Goddess Brid. Please, is there no other way?" Caelan held Rachel, as she buried her face in his chest and weakly pushed Aveline away.

"Ye ken the answer to that as well as I, Laird MacKay. The elemental laws are there for a reason. To protect both gods and man. She must go. But Mannanán Mac Lir loves her and has sworn to be her guardian. Trust me. All will be well." Brid shook her head as she placed her hand on Aveline's shoulder and gently pulled her from her parent's side.

"Join hands with him, Aveline. I will meld ye for all time. The punishment couldha been much worse, child. Ye ken that as well as I." Brid nodded at the god in his human form of the man Aveline had always known as MacCallen.

Sniffing and shaking, with tears coursing down her face, Aveline reluctantly held out her hands. As MacCallen gently cradled her hands in his own, a subtle glow emanated from them. Placing her glowing hands on theirs, Brid bowed her head and their auras immediately merged.

With a smile, Brid released their hands and turned to Harley and Ronan. "Be at peace. Aveline will be happy once again. It will just take a little time." She placed her hand on theirs and the golden rope around their wrists changed into two shining gold rings, one on Ronan's left hand and a matching one on Harley's. As the goddess smiled, a blue-white haze surrounded them. "Through time and space, these two are joined. Fate determined what their union would be. Their souls are now one. Completely intertwined, for all eternity."

As she spoke the last of the rite, she faded from view and the blue-white haze shot up into the sky, clearing the horizon of every cloud. The clan members gathered on the docks and the beach cowered from the shaft of blinding light.

Her form already shimmering and becoming difficult to see, Aveline extended her hands and bathed Ronan and Harley in a loving white light. "I shall learn how to watch over ye whenever ye travel the seas. I promise—when ye need me, I shall be there."

MacCallen nodded, his form also changing as his light merged with that of his precious bride. "Aye, ye will always be protected. That is my gift to my beloved Aveline."

Tears overflowing, Harley slowly shook her head as she watched their lights slowly rise into the sky. "Thank you, Aveline! Without you, I never would've found happiness. You gave me the greatest gift of all."

The wind died down, and the air seemed almost cloying as everyone realized the immortals had finally gone. Harley glanced down at her and Ronan's tightly clasped hands and gasped. Shining black pearls were embedded in each of their wedding bands.

"Hmpf! Fat lot of good it did for me to get dressed in my finest robes just to stand up here like a fixture on this blasted ship." Emrys stamped his staff and eyed the couple with an irritated glare.

With a sad smile at the fuming old man, Ronan bowed his head.

"We would be most honored and happy if ye would also give us yer blessing—since today seems to be destined to have a bit of sorrow mixed with the joy."

Emrys scowled at them and slowly raised his staff. As he nodded their way, the tip of his staff glowed as though energy gathered within the crystal at its tip. "With the strength of the sea and the endlessness of time, this couple before me, I eternally bind. No matter the body, they are of one soul. With each incarnation, their bond will be known."

As he uttered the vow, their rings glowed, and both Harley and Ronan felt as though a growing heat that started in their clasped hands flooded their very beings. Pulling Harley to him, Ronan closed his mouth over hers, and their bodies seemed to meld with the same fiery energy.

The men, women, and children witnessing the ceremony broke into cheers as the couple completed their vows with a kiss. This MacKay wedding would be fodder for a romantic tale to be retold on many a long winter night.

EPILOGUE

Moonlight poured in the bay window, filling the captain's quarters and washing across them as they lay on the feather bed. Deliciously exhausted, Harley nestled her head more comfortably into the dip of Ronan's shoulder and tickled her fingers through the dark dusting of hair across his chest.

He covered her hand with his and ran his other hand up and down her back in a wonderfully possessive way. "Fidgeting, are ye?" He nudged a kiss to her forehead and chuckled. "Did I fail to sate ye, my love?"

"You know better than that." She raised up and propped her head in her hand, but avoided his gaze while worriedly chewing on her bottom lip. A shadow she couldn't ignore nagged at her, stirring worries that this precious happiness that had been so long in coming might be endangered. "I cost you your sister. I worry about that becoming a wedge between us or between me and your family. If not now, then someday."

Without opening his eyes, Ronan tugged her back down and gave her a long, slow kiss. Coming his fingers deeper into her hair, he lifted her face and locked eyes with her. "Aveline's punishment for meddling with the fabric of time couldha been far worse than being bound to Mannanán Mac Lir as his immortal wife. She couldha paid for her poor judgment by forfeiting her existence to the abyss for the rest of eternity."

"The abyss?" Harley ran her hand down his chest, the muscular ridges of his abs, and then lower, pleased to discover he was more than ready to rock the boat again, so to speak. She arched a brow as she straddled him, then leaned forward and wiggled to rub all the right parts against all the right places.

"Lore a'mighty, woman." He groaned and filled his hands with the cheeks of her behind and squeezed. "How can ye feel so wet and ready but still be asking questions?" He lifted her, rocked his hips, and slid inside with a groaning thrust. He groaned again as she started a slow grinding of her hips that matched the gentle sway of the boat atop the waves.

"Maybe since I was such a late starter, I'm making up for lost time," she said, reveling in the way he filled her, the way he hit all the right places and made her feel more alive than she had ever felt before. "You don't mind, do you?"

"Mind?" He rolled her over and settled in with a steady pounding that made his opinion quite clear. He nuzzled her throat and cupped her breast in one hand while rocking into her. "Does this feel as if I mind?"

She raked her nails down his back, then squeezed his buttocks while arching into him. "I am not sure," she dared. "Perhaps you need to drive the point home harder."

He reared up and gave her a wicked arch of his brow. "Drive it harder, ye say?"

She wrapped her legs around him, hugging him with her thighs. "As hard as you can."

"As ye wish, wife—as ye wish." He hammered into her, pounding harder and harder until the gorgeous waves of bliss exploded through her, making her unleash a throaty scream that triggered his answering roar.

They convulsed and shuddered together; him emptying and her

filling until they collapsed and went still except for their ragged breathing.

"There now, love," he rasped. "Is that better now?"

Harley tightened her arms around him and kissed the salty sweetness of his throat. "Much better. As we used to say in Kentucky, that was finer than frog hair split three ways."

Ronan chuckled, then gave her a long kiss before lifting his head and smiling down at her. "I am glad, then, for that is verra fine indeed."

READ ON FOR AN EXCITING EXCERPT FROM:

Beyond a Highland Whisper
A MacKay Clan Legend
Latharn's Story
Book 2

CHAPTER 1

MacKay Keep
Scotland
1410

"Latharn, are ye sure ye never touched the lass?" His father's scowl burned across the room mere seconds ahead of the words.

The reproach in Laird Caelan MacKay's voice stung Latharn like a physical blow. Tension knotted his muscles and his body stiffened with the bitterness pounding through his veins. Only years of respect for his father held his tongue. How could his sire treat him this way? He wasn't an irresponsible boy anymore. How dare he be treated like a lust-crazed lad!

The great hall of the MacKay Keep spanned the largest part of the castle and housed every important gathering of the clan. Flexing his shoulders, Latharn inhaled a deep breath. From where he stood, the room shrank by the moment. He couldn't believe his father had chosen the monthly clan meeting as a means for resolving this matter. How dare he try to shame Latharn into a confession by confronting him in front of his kinsmen. This ploy had worked well enough when Latharn was a lad. His father had used it often whenever he or his brothers had gotten into mischief. Latharn involuntarily flexed his buttocks in remembrance of punishment received after a confession ousted in just such a manner. However, he wasn't a mischievous boy anymore. This was private; they could handle it between themselves.

Every man, woman, and child strained to hear Latharn's reply. His father's closest warriors leaned forward upon the benches. The servants peeped around the corners of the arches, their serving platters clenched to their chests. Latharn rubbed the back of his neck; his skin tingled from their piercing stares.

His father's face flushed a decided shade of purple. Apparently, he'd delayed his answer long enough. Clipping his words just short of blatant disrespect, Latharn growled through a tight-lipped scowl. "How many times must I swear to ye, Father? I have never laid eyes on the MacKinnett lass. I canna bring her face to mind and I havena planted a child in her womb!"

The hall remained silent. Even the dogs sprawling beneath the tables ceased in their endless scuffling for scraps. The only sound breaking the tense silence was the pop of the wood just thrown upon the fires.

With his hands curled into shaking fists, The MacKay pounded the arm of his chair centered at the head of the great hall. Laird MacKay raised his voice to a throaty growl as he edged forward in his chair. "The MacKinnett clan has always been allied with ours. Their lands join our southernmost borders. Must I tell ye how serious these allegations are to our families? The treaty between our clans has been solid for years. God's beard, son! If ye've dishonored their family, there will be no more peace. This lass is the only daughter of their laird!"

His knuckles whitened on the arms of his chair as he continued his tirade. Laird MacKay tensed on the edge of his seat as though he was about to spring upon his prey. His hair heavily streaked with gray, Laird MacKay's once-golden mane gave him the appearance of a battle-weary lion. Though his body showed subtle signs of an aging

Highlander, his eyes still blazed as his roar echoed throughout the great hall.

"Always, ye've been one to skirt danger, Latharn! I will admit...'twas usually for the greater good. However, you yourself must also agree, there have been times when ye have yanked the tail of the sleeping dragon just to see if it would breathe fire. So far, your quick wit has kept ye safe from whatever troubles ye have stirred. But this time, I must know the absolute truth: did ye lie with The MacKinnett's daughter?"

How many times was he going to ask him? Did he think he was going to change his answer? Anger surged through Latharn's veins. Rage flashed through him like a cruel, biting wind. He crossed his arms as a barrier across his chest and curled his mouth into a challenging sneer. They didn't believe him. No matter what he said, they didn't believe his words. He read it in their eyes. He spat his words as though their bitter taste soured on his tongue. "I swear to ye upon all I hold sacred, I don't even know the lass's name!"

A brooding man the size of a mountain stood at Laird MacKay's side. Stepping forward, he thrust an accusing finger toward Latharn's chest as though aiming a lance for the killing throw. "Since when did not knowing a lass's name keep ye from tumbling her in your bed?" Latharn's brother, Faolan, stalked forward upon the dais, shaking his head at his brother's latest scandal. Faolan was the eldest of the MacKay sons, next in line to be laird. The look on his face plainly told Latharn he deemed his brother guilty on all charges as stated.

Latharn snarled. "Stay out of this, Faolan. Ye may have beat the rest of us out of Mother's womb, but ye're no' the laird, yet." Latharn met his brother's glare, squaring his shoulders as he stalked forward to answer Faolan's challenge.

How dare Faolan pass judgment against him? Latharn didn't deny he'd enjoyed many a maid since he'd grown to be a man. However, that didn't mean he'd ever treated them unkindly or shown them any disrespect. He'd sated them fully and when their time was done, he'd taken care to spare their feelings as best he could. Never once had

Latharn been inclined to give of his heart...nor had he pretended to do so just to lure a pretty maiden to his bed.

"The lady's name is Leanna and you will speak of her with respect." The clear voice rang out through the archway of the hall, causing everyone's heads to turn. Latharn's mother, Rachel, emerged from an offset alcove, her eyes flashing in irritation toward her youngest son. "Her clan says she has named you as the father of her child. If she carries your child, Latharn, you will do right by her."

Latharn winced as thunder rumbled in the distance. Whenever his mother's emotions were in an upheaval, the weather's stability always suffered. Rachel's powers directly connected with the ebb and flow of the forces of nature. Her emotions meshed with the energies coursing through the physical realm. Thunder, while Mother was clearly upset, was never a promising sign.

Latharn's heart sank as he heard the ring of doubt echo in his mother's voice. She had always been his greatest champion. Whenever the rest of the family rushed to deem him guilty when trouble was in their midst, Rachel always kept an open mind until she'd heard his side of the story. If his mother already believed him guilty this time, how would he convince the rest of them he didn't even know this lass existed?

Latharn had emerged as the youngest of the MacKay triplets. His name was Gaelic for "the fox" and it had served him well. Little did his parents know how aptly the title would fit when they had chosen it for the innocent babe. Whenever mischief occurred, the wily young Latharn had always been the first to be accused. But that same charm and cunning that was the source of all the mayhem also bailed him out of any trouble he'd caused. That is until now, until this latest uproar that had the entire family in such a stir.

Casting a furtive glance at his mother, Latharn wondered why he was to blame for the women always chasing him. It wasn't as if he went a-whoring all over the country for just anyone to warm his bed. Since he had reached manhood, there didn't seem to be a lass in the Highlands who could resist him. He didn't know why they always sought him out. He didn't do anything special. He was just nice to them...and they followed him to his bed. In fact, sometimes they didn't follow him. Sometimes, he'd find them waiting for him when he arrived in his chambers. Latharn shifted in place and adjusted his kilt. A lass probably lurked in his private hallways this very minute. It had become somewhat of a problem escaping them.

Latharn had grown restless. Now that he was older, he'd grown weary of their freely given charms. A quick tumble with a lass was once an incomparable elation. Now the euphoria had dimmed. The satisfaction had dulled to basic physical release. Even while lying spent in erotic exhaustion with a sated lass cooing by his side, Latharn knew there had to be more.

Of late, he'd found a night spent in a luscious maiden's arms left his heart troubled, as though a question nagged at the tip of his tongue, and the answer danced just beyond his reach. No matter her beauty, no matter her sweetness, they all left him empty and cold. Loneliness settled over him like a weight crushing on his chest.

There had to be more than the mere physical pleasure of losing himself in a woman's embrace. He knew there was more to be found. The security of his parents' love for each other had strengthened their family as far back as he could remember. He sought that glow of contentment he'd seen in his parents' eyes when their gazes met across a room. No matter how many years had passed between them, the look they shared never changed. He ached for the connection his parents had found. He longed to lose himself in another's eyes and speak volumes without saying a word. It was time he cradled his newborn child in his arms, with his loving wife nestled at his side.

Latharn stifled a shudder; the tension gnawed at his gut. The expressions on their faces told him so much more than words. They'd never believe the things he'd done to avoid the women vying for his embrace. His emptiness ached like a festering wound that refused to heal. He had decided to search for the elusive answer by honing his mystical powers. He'd hoped by refining and perfecting his magical gifts, he might solve the mystery of his untouchable heart.

Of late, he'd been so engrossed in sharpening his goddess-given powers, he'd not even walked with a woman in the gardens for several months. He'd been holed up in the northern tower of the keep. There was no way he fathered the MacKinnett woman's child. By Amergin's beard, it had to have been at least five full moons since he'd been outside the castle skirting walls!

The air of the keep closed in around him; the sweltering heat of too many bodies shoved in one room added to his discomfort. Latharn raked his hands through his hair and tore himself from his tortured musings. His mother glared at him, her foot tapping. Perhaps it was the fire that flashed in her eyes bringing the heat to his skin.

"I know of no Leanna MacKinnett!" he ground out through clenched teeth. Latharn braced himself for his family's damning replies. His gut was already wrenched with the unspoken accusations springing from their eyes.

Raking his own hands through his graying hair, Laird MacKay expelled a heavy sigh. Fixing his gaze on his son with a disappointed glower, he dropped his hands to the arms of his chair. "Their *banabuidhseach* will arrive at any moment. Their clan will not be satisfied with your denials until their seer has had a chance to speak with ye and weigh the truth of your words."

Latharn turned to his mother. There was one more thing he had to say in his defense. He didn't care if the rest of the MacKay clan didn't believe him. His mother would believe his innocence.

"Mother! As many abandoned bairns as I've rescued while on my travels, as many waifs as I've brought home to this clan, do ye honestly think I would be able to deny a child of my own blood, a child I had sired? Do ye truly think I would turn my back on a bairn of my very own?"

Latharn towered over his mother, peering down into her eyes and opening his soul to her senses. She had to believe him. He trusted his mother's intuition to see the truth in his heart. His voice fell to a defeated whisper as he groaned and repeated his earlier words.

"I swear to ye, Mother. I am not the father of the woman's child. I know of no Leanna MacKinnett!"

Rachel's hand fluttered to her throat, and she slowly nodded. "I believe you, Latharn. Moreover, I will do what I can to shield you from their *bana-buidhseach*. I hear this woman's powers are amazing, perhaps even stronger than mine. But I'll do whatever I can to protect you from any evil that may be traveling upon the mists."

With a heaviness in his chest and a catch in his voice, Latharn embraced his mother and whispered, "Your belief in me is all I've ever needed, Mother. Ye know I would never bring dishonor to our family or shame upon our clan."

He brushed his lips across his mother's cheek just as chaos erupted at the archway of the hall.

Her shrill cry echoed through the keep as the MacKinnett *bana-buidhseach* screeched like an enraged crow. "I demand retribution for Clan MacKinnett. That heartless cur has sullied Leanna MacKinnett's good name!"

The bent old woman rocked to and fro at the entrance to the hall, brandishing her gnarled walking stick overhead like a weapon.

Her white hair hung in tangled shocks across her stooped shoulders. Her black eyes glittered in her shriveled face, like a rat's beady eyes from a darkened corner. Her somber robes swept the rush-covered floor with every dragging step. Even the brawniest Highlander in the crowd faded back as she hitched her way to the front of the cavernous room.

Drawing a deep breath, Latharn's muscles tensed as the old crone edged her way toward him. Tangible power emanated from her swirling aura as he studied her twisted form. This seer's energies rivaled those of his time-traveling mother. The battering rush of the crone's malicious emotional onslaught threatened to slam him against the farthest wall.

His mother's powers had been refined through several generations to her in the twenty-first century. However, her aura had never emitted such waves of energy, not even after magnification through the portals of time.

Immense anger emanated from deep within this old woman, reaching out toward Latharn like a deadly claw. The crone's soul overflowed with touchable hatred.

Latharn braced himself as a rising sense of dread curled its icy fingers around his spine. He shuddered, swallowing hard against bitter bile as he noticed something else. The *bana-buidhseach's* aura seethed with an underlying layer of evil his mother could never possess. The witch's pulsating energy roiled with a menacing thread of darkness he'd never seen the likes of before.

Cocking her head to one side, a malicious glint shone in her eyes. Her mouth curled into a grimace as she croaked, "What say ye, MacKay cur? Do ye deny robbing my laird's daughter of her precious maidenhead? Do ye deny ruining her for any other man?"

With a single stamp of her crooked staff upon the floor, enraged lightning responded outside, the flash splintering throughout the room. Everyone in the hall cowered against the walls, shielding their faces from the narrow windows high overhead. The acrid tang of sulfur hung heavy in the air from the burn of the splitting energy.

Theatrics to get her point across. This did not bode well. His hands tensing into clenched fists, Latharn took a deep breath before he spoke. "I fear there has been a grave misunderstanding. I have not been outside the walls of Castle MacKay in the passing of the last five moons."

"Exactly!" she spat, jabbing her bony finger from deep within her ragged sleeve. The *bana-buidhseach* hitched sideways closer to Latharn and shook a threatening fist in his face. "Ye appeared to the lass while she lay in her bed. Your vile essence washed over her silken body by the light of the swollen moon. As your spirit swirled upon the mist of the bittersweet night, ye violated her ripe nest and filled her with your seed."

Eyes flashing with a mother's protective rage, Rachel shoved her way between Latharn and the snarling hag. Resting her hand on Latharn's chest, Rachel stood nose to nose with the crone. "Surely, you don't believe in such an outlandish tale? The girl could not possibly find herself pregnant in the way you just described."

The crone hitched her way even closer to Rachel, her dark eyes narrowed into calculating slits. Hissing her reply, her foul breath nearly colored the air around her as she spat through rotted teeth with every word. "Do ye call me a liar, Lady MacKay? Do ye slur the name of Leanna MacKinnett and the honored MacKinnett clan?"

The hall crackled with the conflicting forces of emotional energy as lightning once again splintered the electrified air. Thunder roared, shaking the walls until debris rained down from the rafters.

Rachel circled the wizened old hag. "I've nothing to say about Leanna MacKinnett or the good name of the MacKinnett clan. I defend my son's honor against your lies. I challenge your slander against an honorable MacKay son!"

With a wave of her hand and a narrowed eye, the hag halted Rachel where she stood. The spell she cast silenced Rachel's voice and paralyzed her body. Sliding around Rachel, she stabbed a gnarled finger into the middle of Latharn's chest. A demonic smile curled across her face as she sidled her body closer. With a flourish of one hand, she withdrew a ball of swirling glass from the folds of her tattered robe. Her cackling voice rose to a maniacal shriek as she lifted the ball for all to see. "Do ye deny lying with every maiden whose head ye happened to turn? Do ye deny withholding your heart from every woman in which ye've ever planted your cock?"

Latharn's voice fell to a low, guttural whisper as dread gripped him in his gut. "Who are ye, woman? What is it ye seek from me?" An icy premonition, fear of what was to come, stole the very breath from his lungs. Latharn knew in the very depths of his soul there had never been a Leanna MacKinnett. This wasn't judgment for ruining some woman or the name of her clan. The stench of something much more sinister hung in the air. It rankled with every breath he took.

With a crazed laugh, the shriveled old woman transformed before his eyes. Her dry, tangled hair lengthened into flowing black tresses. Her sallow, wrinkled skin smoothed into creamy silk. Her bent frame straightened, blossoming into a shapely woman, breasts full, hips round and firm.

Her eyes remained black as the darkest obsidian, and her full red lips curled into a seductive, malicious smile. Her voice became a throaty, honey-laced melody, deadly in its hypnotic tone. "Do ye remember me now, my beautiful Highlander? We were together once, you and I. We were lovers, but now I come here as your judge and jailer. And I have found ye guilty of withholding your heart from the only one who truly deserves your love."

"Deardha?" Latharn recoiled from the seductress bearing down upon him.

As she thrust the deep violet globe into his face, Deardha's voice echoed across the hall. "Aye, Latharn. Ye remember me now? Listen closely to my words. I condemn ye to this eternal prison. I banish ye to this crystal hell. Ye are far too powerful a charmer of magic to be toying with women's hearts. No longer will I allow ye to sow your seed with any poor fool who warms your bed. If ye willna pledge your heart to me, then ye shall wish ye were dead." As Deardha uttered the spell, blinding white energy swirled from the tips of her long pale fingers. The shimmering tendrils flowed and curled, constricting around Latharn's body.

With an enraged scream, Rachel broke free of Deardha's binding spell. Forcing her way between Latharn and the witch, she clawed at Deardha's face.

"Mother, no!" Latharn roared, fighting against the tightening bands of the curse meshed about his body. "Ye must get away from her. Save yourself!" He couldn't breathe. His heartbeat slowed and the room darkened around him. This must be what it felt like to die. Latharn struggled to focus his eyes.

The conflicting forces threw Rachel across the room as Deardha's field of malevolence blasted against the walls. The winds howled and roared as the demonic chaos ripped through the castle. Then all fell silent just as swiftly as the storm had risen and a fog of sorrow settled over the room. Latharn shuddered awake to an icy smoothness pressed against his spine. Finding his arms freed, he flexed his hands, wincing as he rolled his bruised and battered shoulders. Where was he? He lifted his head, staring about in disbelief at the see-through globe enclosed around his body.

Everyone eased their way out from where they'd taken cover: they crawled out from under tables, from behind overturned benches.

Eyes wide with fear, they glanced about the room to see if the attack was over.

Latharn spread his hands on the curved, cold glass. What were they doing? Why did they mill around him like he wasn't there? It was as though he sat among their feet on the floor. What the hell were they doing?

The serving lads rushed to re-light the torches lining the walls. The scattered clansmen and villagers rose from the floor, checking each other for injuries. Tables and benches lay about the room like scattered rushes strewn across the floor. Tapestries and tartans hung in tattered strips, nothing left on the standards but bits of colored shreds.

Laird MacKay shoved his way through the wreckage to his wife. Rachel lay in a crumpled heap beside the hearth, her weakened breath barely moving her chest.

"Mother!" Latharn shouted against the glass. If she was dead, it would be no one's fault but his own. Standing, Latharn stretched to see if Rachel would move.

Laird MacKay cradled her against his chest, pressing his lips to her forehead until she opened her eyes.

Rachel struggled to lift her head, her eyes widening with disbelief as she looked across the room directly toward Latharn. Lifting her hand, her voice cracked with pain as she keened her sorrow to all who remained in the great hall. "My baby!" she sobbed. Waving her trembling hand toward her son, she buried her face in Caelan's chest.

Latharn closed his eyes against the sight of his mother rocking herself against her pain. As her wails grew louder, he covered his ears and roared to drown out the sound.

CHAPTER 2

Washington University
St. Louis, MO
2010

"Professor Buchanan, do I get extra credit for fixing you up with him? You know, the fine piece of man we met? That guy we met at last month's conference?"

Nessa Buchanan peered over the top of her laptop, scowling from behind the pair of reading glasses perched on the end of her nose. "If you were one of my students, Ms. Sullivan, you would've just failed the semester for hooking me up with that so-called fine piece of man."

"Oh, come on, Nessa. He couldn't have been that bad." Trish sank her teeth into the apple she'd been juggling as she sauntered around Nessa's office.

After she tossed her glasses onto the desk, Nessa steepled her fingers beneath her chin.

"Trish, do you remember his lecture on the existence of different realities and their definitions as determined by any one individual's perceptions?"

"Vaguely." Trish nodded as she munched another bite of the apple and thumbed through the exams on Nessa's desk.

"Well, it appears that his perception of all night long is my reality of maybe—and I'm really stressing the maybe part—of about, oh, maybe ten minutes."

Nessa stretched across the desk and slammed her hand down on top of the pile of exams. "And after the questionable ten minutes of all night long, he started snoring!" Snoring didn't begin to describe it. He'd practically rattled the windows out of her apartment.

With a grimace, Trish shuddered and tossed her half-eaten apple into the trash. Wiping her hands on the tight seat of her jeans, Trish shrugged. "Come on, Nessa. Was he really all that bad? He seemed kind of nice at the conference."

"He farts in his sleep." Not looking up, Nessa shoved folders of exams into her backpack in a futile attempt at unearthing her disappearing desk. The guy had been a veritable methane gas factory.

"I see," Trish observed with a sigh. "Well, that settles it since we both know you never fart." Trish groaned out loud, as Nessa handed her another stack of exams that wouldn't fit in her already overstuffed backpack.

"And he sucks his teeth," Nessa continued, holding out two more piles of papers toward Trish.

"Before or after he farts?" Trish asked as she juggled the packets of oversized files.

Nessa grunted. "After he eats." Dragging her backpack over into her chair, she huffed as she kneed it shut and wrestled the straining zipper.

Trish backed away from the desk with a defeated shrug. "Okay! I get the message. No more fixups. I'll just leave you to your fantasies about your nocturnal Highlander."

Nessa stopped grappling with her overstuffed backpack long enough to point her finger at Trish. "I will have you know my dreams of my ancient Scotsman have made me what I am today."

The youngest Ph.D. in Archeology at Washington University, Nessa prided herself on the position she'd attained in her field. She'd worked long and hard to get this far, untold hours of solitude, sweat, and tears. She also knew the reason she'd achieved such a lofty position. Nessa owed it all to the inexplicable dreams she'd had since the summer she turned eighteen.

She'd never forget that horrible summer or the catastrophe of her eighteenth birthday. She'd spent summer vacation mooning over the muscle-bound exchange student staying with her mother's best friend.

Nessa realized now she had grown up an insecure child. And no wonder, the way her thoughtless parents had always maligned her with constant criticism.

"Develop what little mind you've got, Nessa. As plain as you are that's all you're ever going to have." Those words had been their constant mantra for as long as she could remember.

However, her mother had noticed Nessa's infatuation with Victor and had plotted a little birthday surprise. The night of Nessa's party, Victor attended her every move. Everywhere she turned, Victor was there. Nessa was delirious. She was thrilled by his touch. She couldn't believe he really liked her. But at the end of the party, the delightful fantasy shattered when Nessa saw her mother hand Victor a check. Her mother then bestowed a pitying smile upon her and told her, "Happy birthday".

Nessa sobbed herself to sleep that night, the night she'd had the first dream. He had appeared as though in answer to her silent cry of despair, this man, this great, hulking warrior the size of a mountain. Soul-piercing eyes glimmered so green and haunting Nessa felt adrift in a sea of pines. High cheekbones, aquiline nose. She sighed. His features had struck her breathless. He had the reddish blond hair that bespoke of Viking ancestry, the strong Norse genetics forged when the marauding invaders overtook weaker villages and sowed their ancestral seeds. At eighteen years of age, Nessa didn't know much about men. But she knew enough to realize this one was pure perfection.

He'd never spoken to her, not a single time. The first time he'd appeared, he'd stood a few steps away as though he didn't wish to frighten her. His gaze had swept across her body, while the faintest of smiles had pulled at one corner of his mouth. The understanding in his eyes had pushed the loneliness from her heart. He'd reached out to her with the barest touch, brushing the back of his fingers across her arm. The trust had telegraphed like electricity across her skin. At last, she'd found someone who wouldn't humiliate her.

As she'd grown older, his repeated visits had changed and evolved into something much more. The dreams had become a subtle courting, a gentle winning of her heart. He'd found clever ways to draw her close, pursue her with a sensitive glance. Always intuitive, he appeared when she needed him. He never pushed her but never failed to respond whenever her subconscious called out. Her Highlander soothed her with his silent caress. He strengthened her with his touch.

She didn't realize her nocturnal visitor was a true Highlander by birth until one of her history classes touched upon the turbulence of Scotland. She'd always loved his unusual garb but had never placed it until one day when she'd opened to a particular chapter in her history book. His kilted plaid fit snugly about his narrow hips as though it were part of his body. His ancient claymore hung at his side as a silent warning. His hand often rested on the hilt as though he found comfort in its touch.

When he'd taken her hand and guided it over the ancient crest pinned at his shoulder, Nessa had fallen hopelessly in love with the man and all things relating to the Scot.

After that, she had been a soul possessed to find out everything she could about Scotland's past. She'd spent months trying to find the elusive crest, in the hopes of identifying her Highlander's clan. She'd found some that were close, but to her dismay, she'd never located an identical match. That's when she'd decided he was just her fantasy. At least if he was only in her head, it meant he could never leave her. Her Highlander would always be hers.

Even though she'd accepted deep in her heart her Highlander couldn't be real, Scotland remained the first love of her life. She studied its history with relentless passion, from its bloody past to its determined people, and how it had changed the course of civilization through the ages. The only drawback of her single-minded obsession, and a rather annoying side effect of her dreams, was the fact that any male met during her waking hours didn't quite measure up against her perfect nocturnal Highlander.

Nessa blamed her continued solitude on the fact that apparently, her parents had been right all along. She must be too homely for any man to consider taking home to meet the folks. That is, any man worth having. Any man like the one in her dreams. There were plenty of them out there ready and willing to participate in messing up the sheets. If you weren't too picky and had approximately ten minutes you didn't mind donating to a total waste of time.

"Nessa! You're doing it again!" Trish dropped a stack of books on the floor.

Nessa jumped, jolted from her reverie.

"I mention dream dude and there you go, off into Nessa-land again."

Fixing Trish with a threatening glare, Nessa tucked her reading glasses into the neck of her shirt. "You drop my textbooks like that again, and I'm gonna recommend you for the Research Department! I haven't forgotten how much you just love disappearing into the archives for days—and nights—at a time."

An opened letter on the desk caught her attention and Nessa's irritation with Trish vanished. "You have to see this! Look! Are you up for an extended trip to Scotland?" Scooping up the paper, she pushed it under Trish's nose, then slung the groaning bag over her shoulder. That multi-folded piece of paper held her magic genie. Her wishes were finally granted.

Trish shook her head as she unfolded the paper. "Come on, Nessa. You know I can't afford airfare to Scotland right now. I'm still up to my eyeballs in student loans from getting my master's degree."

Scanning over the well-worn letter, Trish wrinkled her nose as she read. Pinching the page where her reading had stopped, Trish's face grew thoughtful with what she'd just digested. "Where exactly is Durness?"

Excitement bubbled inside Nessa as though she was a can of carbonated cola. All of her studying and long hours of solitude had led her to the land of her dreams. "Northwestern tip of Scotland. The Highlands. It's finally happened, Trish! I finally got the grant!"

Trish's grin spread into an excited smile as she glanced up again from farther down the page. "This is it? You finally got the grant from the University of Glasgow? This is the one you've applied for three years in a row?"

Snatching the letter out of Trish's hands, Nessa waved it in the air. "You got it, my friend. I finally got the grant. I've received the funding to go on an extended archeological study of the Durness sites and the surrounding areas of Balnakiel. All I have to do is register all of my findings with the University of Glasgow. Anything I find will be tagged by their history department for use in further studies. And since you're my assistant, your expenses are just as fully paid as mine."

"Well then, woo hoo!" Trish hooted at the top of her lungs with a jab of her fist in the air. "That's fantastic! You've been trying to get this grant forever. And Scotland...what is it you call it after you've had about half a beer? The land of your heart's desire? Hey! Maybe you'll meet the great-great-grandson of the guy in your dreams and finally have a sex life worth talking about."

Great. She could always count on Trish to put things in perspective. Nessa laughed as she folded the well-worn letter and forced it into the outside pocket of the backpack. "Tell me, Trish. Why is it you can remember things like that but you can never remember what we've named our database files? And is sex all you think about? I think you're the one who needs to find a guy worth taking to bed."

With a wicked wink, Trish patted her shapely rump before she scooped up an armload of folders off the desk. "I'm not the one who has a problem with snoring, farting, ten-minute teeth suckers taking up space between my sheets."

Buy Here: Beyond a Highland Whisper

MAEVEGREYSON.COM
Magical Romance Sifting Through Time

If you enjoyed this story, please consider leaving a review on the site where you purchased your copy, or a reader site such as Goodreads, or BookBub.

Visit my website at maevegreyson.com to sign up for my newsletter and stay up to date on new releases, sales, and all sorts of whatnot. (There are some freebies too!)

I would be nothing without my readers. You make it possible for me to do what I love. Thank you SO much!

Sending you big hugs and hoping you always have a great story to enjoy!

Maeve

ABOUT THE AUTHOR

maevegreyson.com

Maeve Greyson is a USA TODAY bestselling author, Amazon Top 100 bestseller, Amazon All Star, multiple RONE Award winner, and a multiple HOLT Medallion Finalist.

Maeve Greyson's mantra is this: No one has the power to shatter your dreams unless you give it to them.

She and her husband of over forty-five years traveled around the world while in the U.S. Air Force. Now they're settled in rural Kentucky where Maeve writes about her courageous heroes and the fearless women who tame them. Sometimes her stories are historical romances, time travel romances, or escapist romantasies, but the one thing they always have in common is a satisfying happily ever after. When she's not plotting the perfect snare, she can be found herding cats, grandchildren, and her husband—not necessarily in that order.

ALSO BY MAEVE GREYSON

HIGHLAND HEROES SERIES
The Chieftain - Prequel

The Guardian

The Warrior

The Judge

The Dreamer

The Bard

The Ghost

A Yuletide Yearning

Love's Charity

TIME TO LOVE A HIGHLANDER SERIES
Loving Her Highland Thief

Taming Her Highland Legend

Winning Her Highland Warrior

Capturing Her Highland Keeper

Saving Her Highland Traitor

Loving Her Lonely Highlander

Delighting Her Highland Devil

ONCE UPON A SCOT SERIES
A Scot of Her Own

A Scot to Have and to Hold

A Scot to Love and Protect

HIGHLAND PROTECTOR SERIES
Sadie's Highlander

Joanna's Highlander

Katie's Highlander

HIGHLAND HEARTS SERIES

My Highland Lover

My Highland Bride

My Tempting Highlander

My Seductive Highlander

THE MACKAY CLAN

Blessed by a Highland Curse

A Heartsong Back to the Highlands

Beyond A Highland Whisper

The Highlander's Fury

A Highlander In Her Past

OTHER BOOKS BY MAEVE GREYSON

Stone Guardian

Eternity's Mark

Guardian of Midnight Manor

When the Midnight Bell Tolls

THE SISTERHOOD OF INDEPENDENT LADIES

To Steal a Duke

To Steal a Marquess

To Steal an Earl

Milton Keynes UK
Ingram Content Group UK Ltd.
UKHW021025110624
444053UK00014B/805